"I wasn't questioning that the baby's mine. I was asking if you'd done a test."

"Yes."

"And it was positive."

"Yes."

"Which makes you…" He calculated rapidly. "Six weeks? Seven?"

"Six."

"Right. Time enough for us to get married before you start to show."

Her jaw dropped. "What?"

"You heard. We're getting married."

POSH DOCS

Dedicated, daring and devastatingly handsome—these doctors are guaranteed to raise your temperature!

Meet the doctors who are
the best in the business....

Whether they're saving lives in the hospital,
or romancing in the bedroom, they
always get pulses racing!

HER HONORABLE PLAYBOY

KATE HARDY

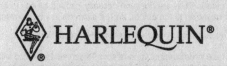

TORONTO • NEW YORK • LONDON
AMSTERDAM • PARIS • SYDNEY • HAMBURG
STOCKHOLM • ATHENS • TOKYO • MILAN • MADRID
PRAGUE • WARSAW • BUDAPEST • AUCKLAND

ISBN-13: 978-0-373-82047-4
ISBN-10:   0-373-82047-X

HER HONOURABLE PLAYBOY

First North American Publication 2006.

Copyright © 2002 by Kate Hardy.

HER
HONORABLE
PLAYBOY

For Phil L, with love

CHAPTER ONE

'JUST why,' Alyssa asked the emergency department charge nurse, 'would I want to win a night out with Sebastian Radley?'

'The real question is, why *wouldn't* you? Hmm, I think there's something wrong here.' Tracey took Alyssa's hand and checked her pulse while looking at her watch. 'Well, you're definitely alive, and your pulse is normal.' She made a show of taking Alyssa's temperature. 'No, that's normal, too—so it can't be delirium.'

'Oh, stop it.' But Alyssa couldn't help laughing.

'How about temporary insanity?' Tracey suggested.

More like Alyssa would be insane to want to go out with Seb. 'No. But I'll give you a donation for the fundraiser anyway.' Alyssa turned the key in her locker, fished out her purse, and took out some money. 'Here. It's for a good cause.'

Tracey raised an eyebrow. 'That's enough for three tickets.'

Alyssa shook her head. 'I don't want any, thanks.'

'But, Alyssa, why not? I mean, the whole reason we're selling tickets is to give everyone an equal chance of winning. If we'd done it as an auction, only the super-rich would be able to keep up in the bidding.'

Alyssa understood that. But there was one big flaw in

Tracey's plan. 'Maybe some women don't want to win a night out with Seb.' Alyssa certainly didn't.

'Why? He's charming, he's witty, he's TDH.'

Alyssa looked blankly at Tracey.

Tracey rolled her eyes. 'Tall, dark and handsome. Honestly. Don't you read the Lonely Hearts columns?'

'I'm not that desperate,' Alyssa said dryly.

Tracey winced. 'I didn't mean it like that. I mean, we all look through them and wonder and... Oh, forget it.' She waved a hand dismissively. 'I know I'm digging myself into a deeper hole here. Seriously, a night out with Seb is worth winning. He knows how to show a woman a good time.'

'Only because he's had plenty of practice.' Alyssa raised an eyebrow. 'In the six months he's been at the Docklands Memorial, he must have dated every single woman in the hospital under the age of thirty-five.'

'Maybe he's just looking for the right one,' Tracey suggested.

'Maybe he's the male equivalent of a right tart.' And Alyssa definitely wasn't interested in someone like him. She'd already learned that lesson the hard way, with Scott Cooper.

Tracey whistled. 'You really don't like him, do you?'

'As a doctor, he's fine.' Thorough, decisive, charming enough to reassure their patients yet at the same time managing to remain detached. Alyssa admired that. It was the way she worked, too. 'But as a date...no, thanks. He's not my type.'

'So what is your type, Alyssa?' Tracey asked. 'I can't remember you ever going on a date in the three years you've worked here.'

Alyssa damped down the stream of impulses—to tell Tracey to mind her own business, to claim that she was gay, to say that she was looking for someone special and would know when she met the right one... Ah, it wasn't fair to take out her bad mood on the charge nurse. Tracey meant well. But the truth was embarrassing, and Alyssa didn't want any gossip about herself doing the rounds. Nobody at the Docklands Memorial Hospital knew about the mistake she'd made, and she intended to keep it that way.

And she didn't repeat her mistakes. Ever.

Sebastian Radley might be charming, handsome and witty—and, yes, she'd admit that he was the sexiest man she'd ever met, with those slate-blue eyes and a mouth that was just designed for sin—but he was a walking disaster where relationships were concerned. Which made him a man to be avoided in her book.

'Hey, I'm a busy medic. I don't have time to date,' Alyssa said lightly. She took a note from her purse. 'Here you go. More hush money. Is *that* enough to stop you nagging me?'

'Hmm,' Tracey said, and smiled. 'Thanks for supporting the fundraiser, anyway.'

And as Alyssa walked away, Tracey filled the registrar's name neatly in on three ticket stubs. *Alyssa Ward.* Their registrar worked far too hard, in Tracey's opinion, and needed to let her hair down. And Seb was just the man to help her do that.

Their consultant, on the other hand, needed to be a bit more serious, to realise that life wasn't just party after party. And Alyssa was just the woman to help him see that.

In fact, Tracey thought, this fundraiser could fix a few problems. All she had to do now was have a little chat with Vicky Radley, Seb's sister, who was joint co-ordinator of the fundraiser. If Tracey could get Vicky on her side, then the Docklands Memorial Hospital was just about to become a much more interesting—and much happier—place.

'This was a really, *really* stupid idea,' Seb informed his sister. 'Remind me again. Why did I agree to do this?'

'Because you just lur-r-rve your picture being in the papers, and the papers love you even more when you're wearing your tux,' Vicky said with a grin. 'The Hon. Sebastian Radley raises money for emergency department equipment: you're guaranteed tons of column inches with this one. Posh but caring. It's a winner.'

'Oh, ha.' He scowled at her. 'Why couldn't I just have made a large donation to hospital funds?'

'Because that's not proper news—it wouldn't have been enough to get the press off Charlie's back. So he'd have ended up trying to sort things out with Sophie while the paparazzi was trying to bang her door down, and she'd have run a mile, instead of agreeing to marry him.' Vicky shrugged. 'It was the best idea I could come up with at short notice. And, may I remind you, you couldn't come up with a better one. You went along with it.'

'Hmm, well. You owe me for this. So does our big brother,' Seb warned.

'Relax,' she soothed, making a last-minute adjustment to his bow-tie. 'You look fantastic. If you weren't my brother and the world's biggest louse to women, I'd be tempted to buy a ticket myself.'

'It was *supposed* to be a promise auction.' Seb's blue eyes narrowed.

'It is, for everything else. But a night with you… Seb, this is a hospital. The debs can afford a bidding war—or, rather, their fathers can—but we need to give everyone a fair chance. That's why we're raffling you instead.'

'If you'd kept it as an auction, you could've bid for me.' He sighed. 'I would have funded you to do it.'

'You'd have bought yourself?' Vicky snorted. 'Oh, come on. Don't expect me to believe that one. You love dating women. You live to party. This is *you* we're talking about.' She paused and gave him a speculative look. 'Unless you've fallen in love and you're going to settle down?'

'Of course not. What do you think I am, stupid?' Seb frowned 'No. I just… Look, I hope those tickets made it clear it was one single night out and not a promise of wedding bells. And that there's absolutely no possibility of an ongoing relationship.'

'Seb, *you're* the prize.' She ruffled his hair. 'Everyone knows the rules.'

'I'd prefer them spelt out, to be on the safe side.'

'Too late. We've sold all the tickets. Just stop fussing, will you?'

'I just hope you pick a ticket for someone matronly who'll love being treated as a star for a night—a make-over, a limo, a swish meal out,' Seb said, his mouth thinning. 'And I'm never, ever, *ever* going to be suckered into doing anything like this again.'

Vicky waited a beat. 'Seb?'

'Yes?'

'Stop being so grumpy, put a smile on your face, and go charm some money out of the crowd.'

Charm. It was what he was good at. And that was the point of tonight after all: raising money for hospital funds. He took a deep breath, and followed his sister's instructions.

By the time he was halfway through the evening, Seb was enjoying himself hugely. He'd persuaded everyone to up their bids just that little bit more. He'd auctioned a professor as a household maid for a day, a charge nurse as a car valet for a week, three Indian head massages, six home-cooked dinners, one very staid head of surgery to wear a silly tie for a week, kisses—one of which he'd bought at an outrageously high price and claimed there and then on the stage, because the nurse who'd promised the kiss was seriously cute—several cakes, four make-overs, two leg-waxes and a case of champagne. The money was just pouring in for the hospital, and the room was humming with expectation and laugher and verve.

This was great. Maybe he shouldn't have been a doctor after all. Maybe he should have been a TV presenter, with the crowds around him like this… Except there was a good chance he'd have ended up in his worst nightmare. Working with kids. Adults, yes; you knew where you stood with adults. But kids? If it was a choice between having his legs plucked—one hair at a time—and working with kids, Seb would choose the plucking. No hesitation.

He was on a high until his sister walked onto the stage with the ward's charge nurse, Tracey Fry.

'This is the moment you've all been waiting for,' Vicky said. 'Tonight's raffle. A night out with the Honourable Sebastian Radley.'

There were cheers, whistles and catcalls. Seb felt his face heat and started calculating the chances of the earth opening up and swallowing him.

The odds weren't good.

'And the winning ticket is…' Vicky had even managed to dredge up a drum roll from somewhere as she turned the tumbler on the drum full of tickets. Oh, he'd pay her back for that.

Tracey opened the little hatch at the top and reached into the drum. She made a big show of digging in deep. And an even bigger show of waving the folded ticket to the crowd.

He'd make *her* pay, too. Couldn't they just get this over with?

Tracey unfolded the ticket. 'Number 457,' she announced.

There was a rustling of tickets and a general murmuring of disappointment.

Please, please, let it be someone who'd take the whole

thing at face value and wouldn't expect his undying love, Seb begged silently.

'Alyssa Ward,' Tracey called.

Alyssa Ward? Seb tried to put a face to the name, and failed.

'Um, Alyssa's not able to be here tonight,' Tracey said.

She wasn't *here*? But… Oh, she must be on duty, Seb realised. Night shift.

'So I'll tell her the good news in the morning,' Tracey added.

'Fix,' someone called teasingly.

Fix? Sebastian didn't like the sound of that. What did they mean, fix?

'The ED can't possibly win Seb for a night. He's staff!' someone else called.

Tracey just laughed. 'That's the luck of the draw. Over to you, Seb.'

He smiled sweetly and pretended to be delighted, and finished auctioning the last few promises. All the while, his mind was ticking over. Alyssa Ward? ED—emergency department—staff?

Ah, yes. *Alyssa Ward.* Their very serious and quiet registrar. He'd worked with her for six months now and still barely knew her. Although she came on team nights out, she always seemed to be sitting at the opposite end of a very long table. Almost, he thought, as if she was avoiding him—but, then again, if she wanted to steer clear of him, why would she have bought a ticket to win a night out with him?

Completely illogical. But that was women for you—his sister excepted. Vicky, Seb thought, was completely logical.

Well, at least he wouldn't have to face Alyssa in the morning. He was on a late—and as she must be on nights, they wouldn't be in the department at the same time. Which would give him a few hours to find out more about her and decide how to play this.

It was one date. And it wasn't even a *date* date. It was going to be fine.

So why did he have this uneasy feeling prickling the back of his neck?

'*You* are going to need full body armour before you go out there,' Fliss told Alyssa, laughing, as Alyssa walked into the ED staffroom and headed for the coffee-machine.

'Full body armour? Why?'

'Because every woman in the hospital's out for your blood today.'

'What?' Alyssa frowned at the nurse. 'Sorry, Fliss, you've lost me completely.'

'You won. Last night.'

Were they in a parallel universe or something? 'Won *what*?'

Fliss groaned. 'You definitely need that coffee to wake you up, Alyssa. You won the night out with Seb.'

Alyssa shook her head. 'Not me. I didn't buy a ticket.'

Fliss raised an eyebrow. 'You must have done. Otherwise how could you have won?'

Alyssa folded her arms. 'I didn't buy a ticket. I gave Tracey a donation.'

'Enough to buy several tickets,' Tracey said, overhearing them and coming to join them. 'So I put your name on a couple of tickets for you. One of them just happened to be the winner.'

Alyssa's lip curled. 'Well, I'm more than happy to donate the prize to somebody else.'

Seb, who'd overheard the last part of the conversation, stopped dead in the corridor. Hang on. Alyssa Ward was supposed to be on night shift—wasn't she?

No. He'd assumed it. Assumed that anyone who'd bought a ticket would have been there to collect her prize, unless she happened to be on duty.

Not only had someone else bought the ticket for Alyssa, she didn't want the prize.

And that *rankled*.

Seb might not want to settle down, but he knew how to give someone a good time. He'd taken Vicky's advice about what to offer. A make-over, dinner in a swish restaurant and good tickets to see a show. What wasn't to like about that?

Clearly, *he* was the sticking point.

He frowned. He couldn't remember the last time someone had refused to go out with him. Actually, he didn't think anyone ever had. This was a first. And he didn't like it one little bit.

So he was going to find out what the problem was. Here and now.

'Why?' he asked, walking into the staffroom. 'Do I have a personal hygiene problem or something?'

At least Alyssa had the grace to blush. 'No. I just don't go out on dates.'

Oh, so *that* was it. And even though he should have been pleased—he hadn't wanted the winner to get the wrong idea and think it meant the beginning of a relationship—her reluctance stung him even more. 'This isn't a date,' he corrected. 'It's a night out, the prize for a fundraiser. A one-off.' And he was annoyed enough to add, 'Oh, and it's tonight.'

To his surprise, she didn't back down. 'What if I'm busy?'

'Then you can reschedule.'

'I think, Mr Radley, *you* can reschedule. Or go on your own.' She looked at him, unsmiling, and put her undrunk coffee down on the table. 'Don't ever try to boss me around again.'

Fliss whistled. 'That's put you in your place,' she said as Alyssa walked off.

Maybe, Seb thought. He'd barely noticed Alyssa Ward before. She was just the quiet, studious registrar he'd worked with a few times—efficient, pulled her weight, good with patients, did her job without complaining, yada yada yada. She always wore plain dark trousers and a cream shirt underneath her white doctor's coat, and he'd barely registered that she was female. She was a professional colleague, that was all.

And he certainly hadn't noticed that stubborn streak. It was an overworn cliché, but maybe her chestnut hair had something to do with it. And maybe she was only quiet because she knew that she had a temper and needed to keep a tight rein on it.

Which made Alyssa Ward a very interesting proposition.

Hmm. They'd have that night out tonight. And he was going to pull out all the stops.

Later that day, Seb had the case from hell. Resus was quiet for once, so he took his fair share of working through the cubicles.

Which meant Seb had to deal with the four-year-old boy who'd caught himself in his zip.

Great, he thought when Mel on Reception handed him the notes. Why couldn't he have had a difficult geriatric, or the six-foot-six body-builder who'd been in a fight and was still drunk and stroppy? But no. He got the kind of patient he found hardest to handle. A kid.

Seb was hopeless with kids. Always had been. Thank God he'd never have to have any of his own. He was only the spare and not the heir to Weston—with any luck, Charlie and Sophie would make a baby really soon and let him off the hook completely.

The little boy was crying and the mum was clearly panicking. Seb switched on his professional smile. 'Come through here with me. We'll soon have him sorted out.'

'He wanted to get dressed himself. I turned my back for two seconds and, and…'

'It's OK. It happens a lot. Little ones forget to put their underpants on, try to get dressed too quickly and catch a bit of skin in the zip.' Oh, please, please, make the boy stop crying. Seb hated the sound of children crying. It went right through him—it was far worse than the sound of chalk squeaking on a blackboard.

'But the zip's jammed! I can't undo it,' the woman said. Her face turned bright crimson. 'And it's his willy! What if it causes…well…problems?'

'It won't,' Seb soothed. 'Trust me, I won't have to do any surgery. I'll give him something to numb the pain so I can manipulate the zip without hurting him any more. Sometimes mineral oil will do the trick—otherwise I'll need to cut the zip, if that's all right?'

'I don't care—I hate the things anyway. His grandmother bought them because she says he looked too scruffy in the pull-up joggers he normally wears. She said he ought to have proper trousers, like they had when my husband was small.'

'Mothers, eh?' Seb said, smiling wryly. Your own mother was meant to be nice and the mother-in-law was from hell. Given what his mother was like, he never wanted to test that theory. The woman who was worse than Mara hardly bore thinking about.

And the kid was still crying. Oh, hell. He hated this. And his attempts at jollying the little boy along clearly weren't working. He needed help. A nurse. Someone who was better with kids than he was. 'I'm just going to get the kit I need. Back in two seconds,' he said, and left the corridor with relief.

The first member of staff he met, he'd beg for help.

He almost—almost—revised that idea when he met said member of staff. But he could still hear the little boy crying. He had to go for the lesser of two evils. And Alyssa Ward was at least cool and calm. She'd be far better with the kid than he was.

He switched to charm mode. 'Alyssa, can I borrow you for a moment, please? I need your help.'

Her eyes narrowed. 'What?'

'Little boy with a zip problem. I need someone to distract him while I do the necessary.' Please, please, let her say yes. Please, let her like kids. Please, let her help me.

She shrugged. 'OK.'

His smile, this time, was genuine. 'Thanks. I appreciate it. Cubicle five. I'm just going to get the lidocaine, mineral oil and cutters.'

By the time he returned—only a few moments later—the little boy was sitting on Alyssa's lap and she was telling him a story. The child was still crying, but he was more interested in the story—something about a train and a dinosaur. Alyssa was a natural, Seb thought.

And then the lightbulb pinged. Of course. Question: why wouldn't you want a swish night out? Answer: when you were married with a small child.

He glanced automatically at her left hand. No wedding ring. Either she didn't wear it at work for hygiene reasons, or she wasn't married but was still committed.

Well, that was an easy one. He'd arrange a babysitter, and she could still have the night out—but with her partner instead of him.

And he could go partying without having to worry about not fulfilling the terms of his promise.

Sorted.

He painted iodine onto the little boy's skin, then slipped in some lidocaine. As the numbing action began to work, the child's sobs diminished and he even started to talk back to Alyssa, asking her bits about the story.

Not wanting to break the peace, Seb quietly told the mother exactly what he was going to do and then worked swiftly in silence. He covered the area in mineral oil—it wasn't enough to make the zip move, so he was going to have to cut the slide. Alyssa was still distracting the little boy, which was good— it meant the child wouldn't worry about the orthopaedic pin cutters which Seb had brought with him.

There was one nasty moment when Seb thought he was going to have to try the other way—using heavy-duty towel clamps on either side of the zip slide and twisting the thing apart—but then the fastener slid apart, releasing the little boy's skin.

Result.

He pulled the exposed zipper teeth open, cleaned the crushed skin and applied some ointment.

'Has your little boy had his tetanus injection?' he asked.

The woman nodded, looking relieved.

'That's good. Now, he's going to be a bit sore for a while, but there won't be any lasting damage. If you're worried about anything at all, call your GP or come back here and we'll take a look.'

'Thank you.'

He smiled. 'Hey, I just did the easy part. Alyssa did the tough bit.' And he really meant it. She'd done the thing he found more difficult than anything else: she'd calmed the little boy right down.

'Thank you, both of you.'

Alyssa brought her story to a swift conclusion, but before she could follow the patient out of the cubicles Seb said softly, 'Alyssa?'

'Mmm-hmm?' She looked faintly wary.

'Thank you for bailing me out.'

'Kids worry you?'

Was it that obvious? 'I'm just… I don't have the rapport with them that you clearly do.'

'No problems.'

He cleared his throat. 'I'm sorry. I didn't realise you were…well, married with kids. Of course you won't want a night out on the town with me. But you won the raffle fair and square, so I'm more than happy to pay for a babysitter as well as the rest of it, so you and your husband can have a night out together.'

She lifted her chin. 'I'm not married.'

'Partner, then.'

Her green eyes glittered. 'And I don't have children. It's just part of my job.'

Hell, she was back to freezing him again. And he didn't like the way she was looking at him. Kind of, well, as if she despised him. And it was irritation that made him say something he knew was seriously stupid, even as he spoke the words. 'Then, if you're free, let's get it over with. Tonight. I'll pick you up at half seven.'

Without giving her the chance to say no, he went to find his next patient.

CHAPTER TWO

ALYSSA really didn't want to go on this stupid night out.

But what choice did she have? If she refused, people would start asking questions. Nosy questions. Dig into things she'd rather keep where they belonged: firmly in the past. Plus, the hospital grapevine would make a big thing about it. For weeks staff on other wards would be pointing her out in the corridors or the canteen as The Woman Who Said No To Seb Radley. Alyssa hated being gossiped about. Been there, done that, absolutely no way in hell she'd ever put herself in that situation again.

And then there was Seb himself. He wasn't the sort of man who took no for an answer—not unless there was a good reason. Which there was, but she didn't want to discuss it with him and have him laughing at her.

So that meant going out with him. Which made her a doormat, for letting other people bully her into doing something she really didn't want to do. Also been there, done that, absolutely no way in hell she'd put herself in that situation again.

Whichever way she looked at it, she lost.

Out of all the hundreds of tickets sold, why had they had to pick *hers* out?

And then a truly nasty suspicion hit her. Tracey had bought

the ticket for her. Tracey—so Alyssa had heard—had been the one to pick the ticket out. Coincidence? Or had it all been a fix?

No. Surely not. Tracey knew Alyssa hadn't wanted the date. It had to be a coincidence.

All the same, it niggled at her.

'Right. Night out with Seb.' Mr Smooth And Charming. It would've helped if he'd told her where they were going when he'd asked her for her address earlier that afternoon. Should she dress up? Dress down? 'Bloody man,' she muttered.

Still, it was just one night. It was a charity thing. So he wouldn't try it on with her; he wouldn't try to add her to the notches on his bedpost. If he did…then she'd remind him about that case they'd worked on today. Toddlers weren't the only ones who could catch themselves in a zip. Especially if they had a helping hand. *That* would be enough to make him realise that she meant business and he was wasting his time.

In the end, she opted for a little black dress and low-key make-up.

At precisely half past seven, her doorbell went.

Well, she supposed that was one point in his favour. He hadn't turned up early, trying to put her on the spot; and he hadn't turned up late, making her stew even more about this whole stupid situation.

She opened the door and her eyes widened.

Seb usually wore a suit at work, but so did the other male consultants. And, sure, she'd seen his picture in the gossip rags often enough, with a woman hanging onto his arm and batting her eyelashes. But she hadn't been prepared for just how good he looked in the flesh, wearing a dinner jacket. Dress shirt. Bow-tie—a proper one, hand-tied, rather than a fake one. Skin freshly shaven. Hair neat. Shoes—hand-made Italian leather which he'd probably bought in Milan, knowing him—perfectly shined.

Everything precisely calculated to make a woman swoon.

Well, she wasn't an ordinary woman. She wasn't going to swoon.

Even if, just for a moment, she would have liked to.

'Hi,' he said.

Then he smiled.

He had a dimple. A *dimple*. How come she'd never noticed it at work? That dimple completely undermined his sophisticated act. It made him look *cute*. And it made her want to reach out and touch him. Just the tip of her finger to the middle of his dimple. From there it would be a tiny, tiny distance to the corner of his mouth. And then tracing the outline of that full lower lip, one that promised the most mind-blowing kisses.

Uh.

She pulled herself together and hoped he hadn't noticed her hesitation. 'Hello, Seb.'

'Ready?'

Not in a million years. 'Sure,' she said, affecting a calm she definitely didn't feel.

'Let's go.'

He had a low-slung sports car. An expensive boy toy. Well, Seb *would*.

'Like the car?' Seb asked.

She shrugged. 'It's got four wheels.' And every bit of chrome was polished to a high sheen. The leather interior was flawless. Clearly it was his pride and joy.

'This,' he said with a grin, 'isn't just a car. It's a vintage E-type Jaguar.'

She couldn't help herself. 'Fancy yourself as James Bond?' Though, she had to admit, he'd make a good James Bond. Smoother than Sean Connery—or Pierce Brosnan, her favourite. Sexier, too.

'No, that'd be an Aston Martin. Everyone remembers the DB5 from *Thunderball*—or maybe you're thinking about the V12 in *Die Another Day*.'

A car was just a car in her eyes—but trust him to know the difference. Still, it could've been worse. She wouldn't have put it past Seb Radley to pick her up in a stretch limo with a chauffeur in full livery.

He opened the door for her. Polite, but not pushy—or maybe he just didn't want anyone else's fingerprints on the car's paintwork.

OK. She could do this. It was just one evening, that was all. Not a date, and there was no future in it. Nothing to worry about.

When Seb had joined her in the car and fastened his seat belt, she asked, 'Where are we going?'

'A quiet restaurant.'

'Not out partying?' She couldn't help the snipe.

He came straight back with, 'Didn't think it was your style.'

A low blow, but she supposed she deserved it.

She didn't say much during the rest of the drive, just let him concentrate on the driving. And he was a good driver. She'd give him that.

The restaurant turned out to be small and discreet, over-looking the Thames. And Seb, of course, had got the best pos-sible table, by the window—just perfect for watching the sky darken and all the lights come out.

'Very pretty,' she said.

He shrugged. 'The food's good.'

The waiter, when he brought them the menu, addressed Seb by name. Clearly it was a favourite haunt of the Hon. Sebastian Radley. The waiter also didn't give her a second look so, equally clearly, Seb must bring a lot of women there. Alyssa was just one in a long, long line.

Not that it should sting. This wasn't a date, and she wasn't interested in Sebastian. There was absolutely nothing to feel upset about. She pushed the emotions back where they belonged. Buried.

This was an expensive place, too, she thought, because there were no prices on the menu. Obviously he intended to impress. Well, she wasn't twenty-five any more. She didn't fall for surface charm. 'What do you recommend?' she asked.

He looked casually down the list. 'It's all good. Order whatever takes your fancy.'

Well, at least he wasn't going to order for her.

'What would you like to drink?' he asked.

She hadn't expected that. 'I thought you'd prefer to order,' she blurted out—and could have kicked herself at the amused look on his face.

'I'm not that much of a chauvinist. I don't know your taste, so I'd rather you picked something you like.'

He was being thoughtful? Maybe she'd misjudged him. 'What about you?'

He shrugged. 'I'm driving, so I'm only having one glass. I'm happy to go with your choice.'

OK. She'd take that at face value. When the waiter came back, she ordered a bone-dry Sancerre and chicken livers with bacon, followed by monkfish.

To her surprise, Seb followed suit.

'I thought you'd be—'

'A red-meat man?' He finished her words, and smiled. 'I like food. All sorts of food.'

That little flicker in his slate-blue eyes meant that 'all sorts' applied to more than just food. Seb was trying to flirt with her.

Well, tough. She wasn't interested in flirting with him, or anything else. As soon as tonight was over, they'd be back to being colleagues—and, as far as she was concerned, the sooner the better.

Even if he was drop-dead gorgeous.

Even if he did have that cute little dimple.

Even if his mouth just invited a kiss.

Seb Radley was trouble, and she'd already had more than enough trouble in her life. She wasn't going to get involved. Not at all.

A woman who knew what she liked. Seb definitely approved of that. He was bored, bored, *bored* with the air-headed debutante type who hung on his every word and expected him to make all the choices.

Alyssa was very far from being an airhead. She was interesting. Though he didn't know the first thing about her—other than that she was very competent at her job and was a lot better at handling kids than he was. And that her eyes were the same shade of green as the sea. How come he'd never noticed that in six months of working with her?

'How long have you worked at the Docklands Memorial Hospital?' he asked.

'Three years.'

She was a bit stingy with information—she was supposed to be chatting back to him. Though he knew it was his own fault for asking a closed question—one that could be answered in a couple of words. OK, Seb. TV presenter mode, he told himself. Put her at her ease—get her talking about a subject we have in common. Which, he guessed, meant their work. 'Have you always worked in emergency medicine?'

'Pretty much.'

'Where were you before the DMH?'

'I moved around a bit.'

Evasive. Hmm. What was she trying to hide? He couldn't tell a thing about her from her accent—there wasn't a trace of a regional burr or upper-class clipped vowels. She was a completely unknown quantity. 'Me, too.'

To his disappointment, she didn't ask him where he'd worked. And she was clearly uncomfortable chatting with him. He let the conversation lapse and just watched her as she stared out of the window. Actually, she was quite pretty. She had a heart-shaped face, a Cupid's bow of a lip—and it was her natural shape, too, given that she was barely wearing any make-up—and those stunning eyes. Her hair was in a short, practical bob, and he found himself wondering what it'd look like when it was tousled. When she'd just woken up. When she was still sleepy and warm and soft and off guard, rather than alert and suspicious.

When the food arrived, they ate in near-silence. The stars were out, the food was good and the waiters were unobtrusive. And his companion wasn't wittering on about nothing and trying to look winsome. This, Seb thought, should have felt perfect.

Except it didn't.

Alyssa didn't want to be here. And she didn't want to go out with him. Not in any way, shape or form. Why?

There was only one way to find out. And he was going to do it her way. The direct way. 'You really don't like me, do you?' he asked.

Alyssa blinked at the question. She hadn't been expecting him to ask that. 'What makes you think that?' she hedged.

'Because you haven't smiled once tonight. Not a genuine smile, anyway.' He frowned. 'So what did I do to upset you?'

'Personally, nothing.'

'What, then?'

He wanted honesty? Then he'd get it. 'It's what you stand for,' she said quietly.

His frown deepened. 'Meaning?'

'As a doctor, you're fine. You do a great job. As a person…' She shrugged. 'Let's just say, if you were a woman, you'd be called some very nasty names indeed.'

'Just as well I'm a man, then.'

His flippancy annoyed her. 'Seb, you just hop from bed to bed. What kind of life is that?'

'Fun, actually.'

She rolled her eyes. 'Oh, please.'

'Want me to prove it to you?' Seb gave her a very, very sexy smile.

One that made her toes curl—or would have done, if she hadn't known it wasn't meant for her personally. He'd have behaved the same towards any woman. Seb was the sort who'd flirt with anything in a skirt—she just bet he'd be able to charm the most difficult geriatric patient, have her blushing and cooing and agreeing to all the procedures she'd just rejected flatly from someone else.

Well, she knew exactly where charming ended up. She didn't want to be there again. 'No, thanks.'

'So you find me unattractive.'

She flushed. 'I didn't say that.'

He pounced. 'So if I'm not unattractive, logically I must therefore be attractive.'

Yes. Seb was physically gorgeous. Not that she was going to inflate his ego any more by admitting that. 'I think you're an egotist. And you hurt people.'

'Egotist, I'll give you. Hurting people, no.' Suddenly the teasing smile was gone from his blue, blue eyes. 'I don't make promises I can't keep. Yes, I sleep with a lot of women. I happen to like sex. A *lot*. But my partners understand the situation right from the start. I'm not going to get married, or live with someone, or have a permanent relationship of any kind.'

'Don't you think that's a bit shallow?'

'Yes. That's me.' He spread his hands. 'Sebastian the Shallow.'

'Now you're making fun of me.'

'No. It's how I am.'

It was her turn to frown. 'So why did you become a doctor? And don't tell me it's because of the reputation of nurses, and it meant you'd get your pick of any girl you wanted. If you were that shallow, you wouldn't have had the dedication to study for as long as it takes to get a medical degree—or have made it to consultant level at your age.'

His face shuttered. 'Medicine just suits me.'

And he wasn't prepared to talk about it. Which meant that the reason was important to him. 'Who's the real Seb?' she asked softly.

He shrugged. 'What you see is what you get.'

She didn't believe him. Somewhere, underneath all that charm, was the real Sebastian Radley. A man she suspected might be a great deal more appealing than Seb the Hon., the socialite. 'I think you're hiding something. Running away from something. You're using all your women as a huge smokescreen.'

'And what are you running away from, Dr Ward?' he riposted.

'Nothing.'

He raised an eyebrow. 'Come on. You've just pinned me down. Because I date a lot, you say I'm running away. You're the opposite: you don't date at all. So what are you running away from?'

Too many memories. Scott Cooper. Her own gullibility. 'That's my business.'

'Uh-huh.' He took a sip of wine. 'Stalemate, I think.'

'Let's drop this,' Alyssa said, suddenly feeling out of her depth.

'You started it.'

True. 'It doesn't mean you have to finish it.'

He grinned. 'I like you. You're refreshing.'

Refreshing? She wasn't sure if that was a compliment or not. 'If that's meant to be a pick-up line, you failed.'

'It wasn't. I'm not planning to have sex with you.'

Her face burned. 'So now *I'm* the unattractive one.'

'Actually, no. Though you're very good at making yourself look invisible. When I heard your name on the winning ticket, it took me a while to place you. You're attractive, Alyssa. Actually, you have the kind of mouth any red-blooded man would want to kiss until your eyes went hazy. The kind of flawless Celtic skin that looks like fresh cream. Skin that just begs to be explored. All over.'

She could just imagine him doing that. Kissing her for hours, until her senses swam and she opened to him. In every sense. Mind, heart and soul—and definitely body. Skin to skin. Feeling his heart beating against hers. Feeling his mouth against her skin, exploring and teasing and finding out where she liked to be touched, kissed.

Oh, hell. She'd thought her defences were sound. Against Seb, they were flimsy. Amateur, even. One more line like that, and she'd be on the point of begging him to take her somewhere quiet.

She dug her nails into her palm, hoping the tiny pain would clear her head. Charming meant cheating. She knew that. She wasn't going to make the same mistake again.

'But there's something else that I always make clear from the start,' Seb said quietly. 'I don't have affairs with women who are married or attached in any way. And I don't try to bully or persuade women into doing something they don't want to do. You've told me you're not interested, and I accept that. I'm not going to push you into having sex with me.'

Alyssa wasn't sure whether she was more relieved or disappointed. Relieved that he wasn't expecting her just to fall into his bed, and disappointed for exactly the same reason.

'Pudding?' He handed her the menu.

When had the waiter appeared? She hadn't noticed. Oh, no. Please, don't say he'd overheard the conversation she'd just had with Seb.

I'm not going to push you into having sex with me.

Her skin burned with mortification.

'I,' Seb said, keeping his gaze firmly fixed on hers, 'am having *crème brûlée.*'

Crème brûlée. Celtic skin that looks like fresh cream. He was doing this on purpose.

She glanced at the menu. 'It's not on the list.'

He smiled. 'They'll do it for me.'

His arrogance was breathtaking. On the other hand, if he was a regular customer—a *very* regular customer—the staff probably indulged him.

That was Seb's trouble. He was over-indulged.

'Not by everyone,' he said, and her hand flew to her mouth.

'I didn't mean to say that out loud,' she muttered. 'Sorry.'

'If you were anyone else, I'd demand a kiss as a forfeit.' He leaned back in his chair and gave her a lazy grin. 'But you're not interested.'

'Quite right.' *A kiss as a forfeit.* Her whole body tingled at the idea, but she forced herself to sound cool, calm and collected. 'I'll have the lemon posset, please.'

Though when their desserts came, she wished she'd asked for *crème brûlée* as well. It looked gorgeous. The perfect caramelised crust—and with a raspberry on the top, dusted with just a smidgen of icing sugar and decorated with a tiny fresh mint leaf.

Clearly her longing showed on her face, because Seb scooped the raspberry from the top of his pudding, and leaned over towards her. 'Open wide.'

'I...'

Another hint of that, oh, so sexy smile. 'You know you want to.'

Oh, yes.

She opened her mouth and allowed him to feed her the mouthful of fruit, caramel and cream.

'My turn,' he said softly.

He wanted a taste of her pudding?

Oh, Lord. If this was 'not pushing', she hated to think what he'd be like when he *was* trying to persuade someone into having sex with him.

Frankly, he wouldn't even need to try. If they weren't in the middle of a restaurant, she knew she'd be taking her clothes off right now and letting him do whatever he liked. Because she knew he'd make it good for both of them.

Embarrassed, she scooped a spoonful of the lemon posset and fed it to him.

He licked a smear from his lower lip, making her temperature rise a notch. 'Creamy and smooth, with a hint of tartness. My idea of perfection,' he said.

He was talking about the dessert. So why did she want him to be talking about *her*?

Somehow she managed to keep her composure during the rest of the meal. Coffee and tiny petits fours. When they'd left the restaurant, Seb switched on his CD player and she pretended to listen to Mozart so she wouldn't have to make conversation on the way back to her flat.

And then a car overtook Seb in the middle of a roundabout. A small, bright yellow car—at least, the bits that weren't rusty were yellow. The exhaust sounded illegal and the music pumping from the car was so loud that they could actually hear it above the music in their own car—and their windows were closed.

'Idiot!' Seb yelled, then glanced sideways at Alyssa. 'Sorry.'

'It *was* a stupid place to overtake,' Alyssa said. 'But let it go. Don't get into a boy racer match.' She could imagine Seb chasing after the yellow car and overtaking it, just to prove that he could.

'I'm not *that* immature,' Seb said. 'I get it all the time in this car—people either want to drive it or want to beat it. But I also know this car could take on just about anything on the road and win. I don't have to prove anything.'

All the same, when they came to the next set of traffic lights, the yellow car was next to them.

The driver—who looked young enough for it to be his first car, *if* he was even old enough to drive it—spread his hand as widely as he could and waved manically at them—with the kind of wide smile Alyssa associated with the more over-the-top children's TV presenters. What was going through his head was obvious: *Look at me! I'm king of the road—I overtook you and your flash car!*

Seb revved his engine.

'As you said, you're not *that* immature,' Alyssa reminded him.

'Yeah.' He grinned. 'Though if you weren't in the car with me, I'd be tempted.'

She could just imagine it. 'Well, don't.'

Seb pulled away sedately, but the young driver of the yellow car wasn't going to let it go. He screeched in front of Seb without indicating, jammed his brakes on—hard enough that Seb had to brake sharply, too—then roared off.

Seb swore. 'Teenage showing-off I can ignore—but that was downright dangerous. I need a word with that kid.'

'Leave it, Seb. Walk away.'

Seb shook his head. 'I don't care if he's got a car full of yobs with him. He needs to know that what he's doing is going to end up in an—'

Just as he was about to say the word, it seemed to happen in slow motion. The yellow car was still speeding, and the driver appeared to be concentrating more on what was going behind him. That, or he just didn't see the red light.

Or the lorry pulling out of the junction.

CHAPTER THREE

ALYSSA was already reaching for her handbag as Seb said, 'Call the emergency services.'

She gave the operator their location, then explained what had happened. 'Collision between a car and a lorry. Four in the car, not sure about the lorry. They might need to be cut out, so we'll need the fire brigade as well as at least two ambulances and the police.' She finished giving the necessary details and followed Seb over towards the crash site—he'd already taken a bag and a torch from the boot of his car.

'That isn't a trauma kit, by any chance?' she asked hopefully, as she caught him up with him.

'First aid only.' He blew out a breath. 'The best we can do here is triage and sort out minor wounds until the paramedics get here.'

The bonnet of the yellow car had been pushed back into the car, though the vehicle had slewed on impact so the brunt of the impact was on the driver's side. The lorry driver had climbed out of the cab—so at least that was one less person to worry about, though Seb made a mental note to check him over too. With collisions, sometimes the injuries weren't apparent straight away. There could be something nasty storing itself up.

'We've called the emergency services. We're both doctors,' Seb said. 'This is Alyssa and I'm Seb. Are you in any pain at all?'

'No. But where the hell did they come from? I didn't see them!' The lorry driver was shaking—whether from fear or anger, Alyssa wasn't sure. 'Bloody joy-riders! The lights were green my way. I wouldn't have pulled out if it wasn't clear.'

'They went through a red light,' Seb said quietly.

'It wasn't your fault,' Alyssa said. 'Look, can you sit down over there? We'll check you over when we've had a look at this lot.'

'I'm all right.' The lorry driver looked at the car. 'Oh, hell. The driver's never going to get out of that alive.'

'He's alive now,' Alyssa said, 'and we're going to try to keep him that way. And even if you feel fine now, we still need to check you over.'

'Is there anything we need to worry about in the lorry?' Seb asked quickly.

The driver shook his head. 'My load's just fruit.'

So they didn't have to deal with the risk of a chemical spill on top of this, Seb thought with relief. Good.

The driver of the car was crying as they went over to him. 'Don't hurt me, don't hurt me. I can't get out. I'm stuck. Don't hit me!'

Did the driver *really* think he was going to beat him up for overtaking him? Seb wondered. That he'd smash his fists into a young lad who was stuck in a crushed car and couldn't defend himself? Hell, what sort of life had the kid led? 'I'm a doctor,' Seb said calmly. 'And it looks as if you're hurt enough.'

'Let me handle this,' Alyssa said softly.

'I know I was stupid,' the driver said, his voice shrill with panic. 'I was showing off. I'm sorry. My mum's going to kill me.'

Seb, noting the state of the vehicle, sent Alyssa a speaking glance: the boy's mum might not get the chance. If there was a penetrating abdominal wound, or if the inside of the car had caused severe crush injuries, they'd be lucky to get the driver out alive.

'It's OK,' Alyssa said. 'You need to keep calm, so we can get you out of there.'

The driver gave Seb another scared look, and Alyssa nudged Seb. Hard.

'I'll check on your mates,' Seb said quietly. 'You hang on in there. Alyssa's going to look after you.'

'What's your name?' Alyssa asked.

'Gavin. My mates call me Gaz.'

'I'm Alyssa. I'm a doctor, too. I'm going to try and help you.'

'I'm so scared!'

He couldn't be more than eighteen, Alyssa thought. 'It's OK, love. We'll get you out of there. Can you tell me where it hurts?'

'My arm.'

'Anywhere else?'

'No.'

This wasn't good. From the state of the car, Alyssa knew Gaz's legs had to be crushed. If they weren't hurting, that was a bad sign: it meant there could be severe nerve damage.

'You said you were stuck. Where are you stuck—your arm, your legs?'

'My legs.'

Probably his feet were jammed underneath the pedals. 'Can you move your left foot for me?' she asked.

Gaz began to shake. 'No.'

'How about your right?'

'No. I can't feel anything.' Then his eyes widened as realisation hit him. 'Oh, God, I can't feel my legs!'

'It's OK,' Alyssa soothed, knowing it was very far from OK. If this was a crush injury, the chances were that Gaz was already bleeding to death—or that the pressure of the car against his legs had stopped the blood flow. Which meant that the second they cut him out and the pressure was released, he'd start to bleed heavily. As it was, there was a risk of compartment syndrome, where his blood would compress the nerves and muscles and the blood wouldn't go through the tissues properly—so he could end up with a lot of dead muscle tissue.

If he survived that long.

Don't think about that, she reminded herself. Concentrate on saving him, not on the poor odds. Go through the drill. ABCDE. Airway fine—obviously no obstruction because Gaz could talk. Breathing fine—no pallor, no blueness around the lips, no rasping. Not a tension pneumothorax at this stage, then, though she'd need to keep a close eye on him and act the second she noticed any of the signs. Circulation was the one she was really worried about: if Gaz had a large external haemorrhage, it was going to be hard to staunch it.

But the streetlights weren't enough to show her what she needed to know. 'Seb, can I borrow your torch a minute?' she called. At the same time, the rest of the mnemonics were going through her head. Disability—Gaz was awake and responsive, so neurological worries could be put aside for now. Exposure—well, they couldn't move him until the fire brigade cut him out, so no point in worrying about that one.

Airway, breathing—her breath hitched—circulation.

Seb appeared with the torch. Alyssa shone it into the car. The light told Alyssa that what she'd most feared wasn't there: no dark patch of blood spreading across Gaz's seat.

If only the ambulance and fire crew would get here. Like yesterday.

'Are my mates OK?' Gaz asked.

'Hold on there a second, and I'll check with Seb,' she said, and pulled Seb away from the car. 'We need to get him out of there, fast. I'm not sure if we're going to have time to get him cut out of the car.'

'Bad haemorrhage?'

'No, but probably crush syndrome.'

'So the second we move him, he's going to crash,' Seb said.

'We are *not* going to lose him,' Alyssa said in a fierce whisper. 'I'm going to try and keep him talking. He wants to know about his mates.'

'Tell him that one of his mates was knocked out briefly so he needs to go in to be assessed, and the two in the back have whiplash and will be fine. I'll check the lorry driver and I'll be back.'

Alyssa went back to Gaz, who'd grown paler and more frightened. She held one of his hands. 'OK. Seb says your mate in the front was knocked out, so we'll check him over at the hospital. The two in the back have got whiplash but they'll be fine—they just won't be up to going clubbing or playing football for a couple of weeks. Seb's checking the lorry driver, but he managed to get out of the lorry all right.'

'Oh, God. He must be so mad with me.'

Yeah. And he'd be giving a statement to the police. So if Gaz had stolen the car and gone joy-riding, the police would throw the book at him. But that was the least of their worries right now. 'It's OK,' she soothed. 'The fire brigade is on its way and we'll get you out of there.'

He shivered. 'I'm cold.'

'Hang on in there, Gaz. Do you want me to call your mum?'

'I can't reach my phone.'

'It's OK, I'll use mine.'

'I'm so scared,' he whispered.

'I know, love. I would be, too. But the lorry's stable and it's not going to fall on you, and the fire brigade will cut you out and lift the car off you. I've seen it lots of times before.' And she'd coped as part of the trauma team in a major motorway pile-up. Several times. But this…this was different. It felt *personal* somehow. 'Tell me your mum's number and I'll get her for you.'

But when Gaz had finished dictating the number and Alyssa had made the connection, the network message informed her that 'this person's mobile phone is switched off'.

'She's gone out, then,' Gaz said. 'Am I going to die?'

That depended on the crush injuries, but if she told him that, he'd panic. She needed to keep him as calm as possible. If he panicked, it would send his blood pressure up and cause more problems. 'I hope not. How old are you, Gaz, twenty?'

'Eighteen. Passed my test last week—first time,' he added, with a hint of pride in his voice. 'My old man bought me the car.'

So the lorry-driver had been wrong. Gaz *wasn't* a joy-rider. Good. 'Do you want me to call him, or is he with your mum?'

Gaz shook his head. 'He doesn't live with my mum. Never has. And he only bought me the car 'cause he thought it might stop her going on about the child support he owes her and never paid.'

Oh, yeah. She knew all about that one. A dad who didn't give a damn and thought he could buy his way out of his responsibilities. Her teeth gritted.

'I'm not going to walk again, am I?' he asked.

'Until we get you out of there, we can't assess the damage,' she hedged.

To her relief, before Gaz could ask the crunch question again—was he going to die?—the fire brigade arrived.

'Don't leave me,' Gaz begged. 'Please, don't go.'

'Of course I won't. But I might have to get out of the way for a few minutes while they cut you out, OK?'

He nodded weakly. Seb had clearly briefed the fire brigade. When they asked her to move aside, she went over to where he was briefing the paramedics and gave them Gaz's obs.

'We've done all we can here,' Seb said, when she'd finished.

Alyssa shook her head. 'Gaz is panicking like hell. He asked me not to leave him. So I'm staying.' She bit her lip. 'As soon as they're ready to take that car off him…'

'Hey. There's still a chance. A small one, but there's still a chance.'

Not much of one, and they both knew it.

'I said I'd get his mum for him.' Alyssa hit the redial button on her phone. Ten seconds later, she cut the call. 'Her phone's still switched off.' She turned to the paramedics. 'The driver asked me to stay with him—he's pretty scared. Can I go with you and hold his hand? It'll help keep him calm. Plus, I'm a doctor in the ED at Docklands Memorial, so I can help out in the back as well.'

To her relief, they agreed.

'I'll meet you at the hospital and take you home,' Seb said.

She shook her head. 'Don't put yourself out.'

'Alyssa, don't argue. I'm not going to see you stranded at the hospital or having to wait hours for a taxi.'

Both were distinct possibilities—possibilities she didn't relish—so she wasn't going to argue with him. 'Thank you.'

She went over to the paramedics and held Gaz's hand as they strapped him to a spinal board. They soothed him, but Alyssa had noticed the momentary tightening of their faces before they'd masked their expressions. They didn't think he had much chance either.

'I tried your mum again but couldn't get her,' she said softly.

'If I d… If I don't make it,' he choked, 'will you tell her I love her and I'm sorry?'

She forced the tears back. No time for emotion now: she had to be a professional. And if she told him the truth, what would it achieve? She'd just make his last few minutes as miserable as possible. 'Sure, but you'll be able to tell her yourself.' If she could get Gaz's mum on the phone. 'We're getting you out of there.'

'Will you go with me in the ambulance?'

'Of course I will.'

And then it was the bit she was dreading. They lifted the car off Gaz, applied direct compression to his crushed legs and rushed him into the ambulance.

Seb finished giving his witness statement to the police, then climbed back into his car and drove to the hospital. Thank God he'd thought straight enough to ask which hospital they were going to rather than just assuming it was the nearest one.

He hadn't planned tonight to be like this at all. It should have been fun, a night out, a good meal, and nothing more than that.

And the whole thing had turned into a nightmare. If they'd left five minutes sooner or five minutes later, Gaz and his mates wouldn't have seen the E-type and behaved so stupidly. Probably egged each other on: *Go on, Gaz, you can take it, give it some va-va-voom!*

And Gaz wouldn't be in the back of an ambulance right now with crushed legs—legs that might well have to be amputated.

If the kid even made it to the hospital.

Alyssa had been amazing. Cool, calm, collected and kind—she'd done all the right things in the right order. She hadn't even worried about the fact that doctors' professional indemnity insurance didn't cover them at the scene of an accident, unless they were there on a shout as part of their job. And she'd cared enough to go with a frightened teenager in the back of an ambulance, holding his hand and reassuring him.

There was a hell of a lot more to Alyssa Ward than met the eye. And Seb found himself wanting to know more.

Seb parked the car and headed straight for the emergency department. Alyssa was sitting in the reception area, talking to a policeman—clearly giving him a witness statement.

He waited until she'd finished and walked over to her. She looked drained and miserable—drained because she'd done so much to keep their patient going, and miserable because she wasn't staff and could do absolutely nothing to help the boy now. He knew exactly where she was coming from, so he wrapped his arms round her and held her close.

'He's in Resus. Critical,' she said, her voice shaking.

'Hey. You got him here. That's a hell of a lot better than we hoped for.'

'He's only eighteen, Seb. He made a stupid mistake, yes, but he's so young!'

'I know.' He stroked her hair. 'I feel bad now. I was going to chase after him and yell at him.'

'Maybe if someone had done that before…' She added bitterly, 'His dad didn't bother to stick around and help guide him. What the hell is *wrong* with men?'

Seb knew that wasn't a dig aimed at him—he had a feeling it went far deeper than that. Did Alyssa have issues with her father? Then again, he thought wryly, they couldn't be much worse than his own issues with his mother.

He said nothing, just held her until she'd calmed down enough to pull away.

'Before you say it,' he said softly, 'that was a professional hug. That was a "we've got a patient critically ill in Resus and it's a bad day" hug from one doctor to another. An "I know how you feel because I've been there" type of thing. No strings, no expectations.'

She didn't say anything, but the hard look in her eyes softened.

Did she really think he was that much of a louse—that he'd see she was emotionally drained and use it as a lever to get her into bed? Is that what everyone else in the hospital thought of him?

Suddenly, Seb didn't like himself very much.

'Look, you can't do anything else for him now. We're not staff—not here,' he said. 'Let's call it a day. Go home, get some rest. And ring in tomorrow.'

'And they'll tell me he's "comfortable". Patient confidentiality,' she said bitterly.

'Explain who you are. And if that doesn't work, I'll lean on the consultant for you,' he said.

She didn't look convinced. 'Alyssa, if you stay here all night, he might still be critical in the morning,' he said gently. 'You need to get some rest. Come on.'

They drove back to her flat in silence.

'Thank you for tonight,' she said stiltedly.

'Thank *you*,' he said. 'And I'm sorry.'

'The accident wasn't your fault.'

'I didn't mean that.'

She frowned. 'What, then?'

She already thought the worst of him, so she may as well know the truth. 'This night out was supposed to be a make-over for you, dinner and a show. Except it annoyed me that you were throwing it back in my face—so I decided on the spur of the moment to make you go out with me *tonight*. Which meant I didn't have time to get tickets for a show or organise a make-over.'

That was the last thing she'd expected from him. A confession—*and* an apology. Despite her misery—and the fact that she felt so very, very cold—she smiled. 'You're admitting to being a spoiled brat and having a temper tantrum?'

'Yep.' A hint of dimple. 'Forgive me?'

And then she realised what he was doing. Charming her. She'd say yes; he'd ask for a kiss to prove it; and, the next thing she knew, she'd be inviting him in for coffee. No—worse than that. She'd be inviting him in for sex. Partly because she found him attractive, and partly because, after the accident they'd just helped to deal with, she needed to celebrate life.

Hell. Not *this* way. Not a one-night stand with Seb Radley.

'Nothing to forgive,' she said, and unclipped her seat belt. 'Thank you for dinner.'

'My pleasure.' His expression was odd, unreadable.

'Goodnight,' she said, and climbed out of the car before he could come round and open the door for her.

As if he guessed why, he stayed put and didn't suggest seeing her to her door. Though she noticed that he waited until she'd unlocked her door, switched on her light and closed the door again behind her before he pulled away. Politeness? Genuine concern? Or just hoping that she'd change her mind and make an offer?

She wasn't sure which. Maybe a bit of all three.

One thing she was sure about. Sebastian Radley had the power to unsettle her, if she let him. So she'd keep her distance in future.

CHAPTER FOUR

SEB couldn't sleep. It wasn't the accident—he'd seen far worse in the emergency department. Years of working in emergency medicine had taught him that you couldn't save everyone: you did your best and accepted everything else.

No, it was Alyssa.

She was the first woman he could remember not being able to charm. Which in itself was annoying. And then there was the fact that she'd been sharp enough to guess that he was hiding something. She was hiding something herself, too, he thought—maybe a past relationship, and definitely issues with her father.

Ah, hell. He had to get her out of his head. He wasn't in the market for a long-term relationship, and Alyssa wasn't the type who was up for something short term. She didn't even like him very much.

What he needed was a distraction. Preferably blonde and cute, with an hourglass figure. Tomorrow, he'd start looking.

'How did it go, then?' Tracey asked. 'Did you have a good time?'

'It was OK,' Alyssa said coolly.

'A night out with Sexy Seb, just *OK*?' Fliss asked. 'Come off it! Where did he take you?'

'Dinner.' At Fliss's uncompromising stare, Alyssa added, 'In a restaurant overlooking the Thames.'

'What did you have?' Tracey asked.

Alyssa chuckled and added milk to her coffee. 'What is this, an interrogation? I had chicken livers, monkfish and lemon posset. And the food was very nice.'

'And?' Fliss prompted.

'And that's it.'

'Seb just took you home?' Tracey sounded disappointed.

'Actually, we ended up in the emergency department at Albert's.'

'*What*? Are you all right?' Fliss asked.

'Yeah. Fine. We stopped to help at an accident.' Alyssa's jaw tightened. 'Teenager, just passed his test, went through a red light and hit a lorry. Crush injuries.'

Tracey winced. 'Please, don't. That makes me think of Michael.' Tracey's son was seventeen and driving her crazy with requests to put him on the insurance for her car and take him out between driving lessons. 'Did he make it?'

Alyssa grimaced. 'He was critical last night. I rang this morning and—after I'd explained who I was and that it was discussing a joint patient, not breaking confidentiality—the hospital said he had a good chance, but he's lost both legs. Poor kid.'

'That's a hell of an end to an evening. Maybe you ought to make another date, to make up for it,' Fliss suggested.

'I don't want to go out with Seb.' He was an excellent doctor, and he had a good heart—the fact that he'd met her at the hospital last night instead of making her find her own way home proved that. But she also knew his reputation. Seb didn't do more than one date—a date that usually ended up in his bed. And Alyssa didn't want to be a notch on his bed-

post. 'And just stop trying to matchmake, you two,' she added,
trying to keep her tone light. 'It's not going to work. For a
start, Seb likes leggy blondes and I'm not one.'

'Nothing that a bit of peroxide couldn't fix,' Tracey said
with a grin. 'My Kelly's nearly finished her hairdresser and
beautician training. Just say the word and I'll send her over.
In fact, she could do you hair extensions, so you could do the
"tossing your hair over your shoulder" bit.'

'No. Absolutely not,' Alyssa said, laughing. 'I'm fine as I
am. But thanks for the offer. I think.'

She was still smiling when she went to cubicles to see her
first patient. As if she'd have a second date with Seb. The first
one had only been because of a raffle ticket. They had nothing in common, apart from a career in medicine. Oh, and
maybe the same taste in puddings—but that was it. Plus, Seb
never did more than one date. And she was happiest on her
own anyway.

But, later that day, she was faced with a case she really
didn't like. The mum was convinced it was bad nappy rash
but the creams hadn't been working. 'But she's in pain. I
can't keep giving her baby paracetamol for nappy rash! I
asked my friend, and she said it looked as if I'd put Daisy
in a bath that was too hot. But I didn't. I've read all those
stories about babies falling into hot baths, so I always put the
cold water in first and add the hot, then check it with my elbow.'

'You've done the right thing, bringing her in here, Mrs
Steward,' Alyssa said. She gently undressed the baby and
opened the nappy, wincing as she saw the large red sore areas.
'I can see what your friend means. It's one of two things, but
my guess is that it's scalded skin syndrome.'

'I just told you, I'm careful with her bath! And I'm the one
who bathes her—my husband's always working late. He

hardly even *sees* her. I'm the one who cares for her all the time. And I didn't do anything wrong!'

Mrs Steward's voice had risen to a shriek. Oh, hell. Alyssa needed to calm the woman down right now. 'Of course you didn't do anything wrong. It's just a name for a medical condition. It's caused by a bacterium called Staphylococcus.'

'Bacteria? But I always change her frequently. Really frequently. We use those green nappies—the washable ones—and I wash them exactly as I'm supposed to do. It's *not* because I'm dirty.'

'Of course you're not,' Alyssa soothed. 'It happens when the baby has an infection—usually something in the nose—and the bacterium gets into her system. Children's immune systems aren't as strong as adults', so they pick up more bugs.'

Mrs Steward was shaking. 'I didn't do anything wrong.'

'I know.' Alyssa didn't usually have problems dealing with parents. But she had a feeling that there was more to this than met the eye: the baby wasn't much more than six months old. Which meant that the mum could have postnatal depression—depression that hadn't been picked up because she'd seemed so good at coping. And hadn't she said that her husband was always working late? If she wasn't getting support from her partner, she was probably getting near the point where everything could implode. Without warning.

'Would you mind if I checked something with one of my colleagues?' Alyssa asked. 'Simply that this redness might be another skin condition or another virus. The treatments are different so I want to be sure of my diagnosis.' She was pretty sure of her diagnosis, that it was staphylococcal scalded skin syndrome rather than scarlet fever or toxic epidermal necrolysis. When she'd rubbed one of the red areas very gently, the skin had peeled off in a large sheet—known as Nikolsky's sign. The raw area left behind would dry out and crust over. But she also needed someone who was good at calming women down.

And only one person would do. Seb.

Mrs Steward gave her a searching look.

'If you'd like to do Daisy's nappy up and wrap her in the blanket to keep her warm, I'll be back in a second.'

To Alyssa's relief, Seb was just heading towards the reception area when she pulled the cubicle curtain closed behind her. 'Seb. Got a minute, please?'

He looked at her, surprised. 'Problem?'

'Yeah.' Alyssa kept her voice low. 'Look, I know you hate babies, but I don't need you for Daisy.'

'Daisy?'

'The baby. I need you for the mum—Mrs Steward.'

He frowned. 'I'm not with you.'

'She's very jumpy—everything I say she's taking as an accusation. I'd say she might have postnatal depression that hasn't been picked up, especially as it doesn't seem as if she's getting the support she needs at home. And I need someone to help me with her so I can treat the baby.'

'What's up with the baby?'

'SSSS. But I think she'll take the explanation better from you than from me.'

'Sure it's not TEN?'

Toxic epidermal necrolysis, which had very similar clinical features to staphylococcal scalded skin syndrome, was usually caused by a bad reaction to a drug. 'I don't think so. But I haven't had a chance to ask her if the baby's had any drugs other than nappy rash cream or infant paracetamol.'

'OK. I'll come and have a word.'

'Thanks.'

* * *

Seb followed Alyssa into the cubicle, feeling oddly pleased that she'd asked for his help. 'Hello, Mrs Steward. I'm Seb Radley, ED consultant,' he said, holding his hand out to the worried-looking woman cuddling her baby.

She took his hand and shook it. She didn't offer her first name, though, he noticed. Not that he thought he was God's gift to women exactly, but usually they responded to him. Hmm.

'Alyssa tells me she thinks Daisy has a condition called staphylococcal scalded skin syndrome. May I take a look at her?'

Mrs Steward gave him a suspicious look, then nodded, un-wrapping the blanket from Daisy. Seb gently undid the nappy and took a look at the reddened skin. 'Can I ask if Daisy has had any medication? This soreness might be a reaction to the first time she's had a drug,' he said.

'Only baby paracetamol and nappy-rash cream.' Mrs Steward blanched. 'Could *I* have done this to her?'

'That's extremely unlikely,' Seb said. 'Alyssa's going to take a little sample from Daisy's nose and her skin so we can send them to the lab for analysis. I promise it's not going to hurt her.'

'So what is it?'

'It's something called staphylococcal scalded skin syn-drome—sometimes you might hear people talking about Ritter-Lyell disease. It's the same thing. Would I be right in saying it's only been like this for a couple of days?'

'She had a couple of, well, scaly bits around her nappy area. My mum said it was probably nappy rash, so I put some cream on. But it got worse.'

'And you did exactly the right thing, bringing her here,' Seb said. He gave Alyssa a quick nod, and was relieved to see she was quick enough on the uptake to take the sample while he was talking to Mrs Steward. 'I bet she's had a bit of a runny nose lately, too.'

'Well, yes.'

'What happens is that a bacterium called *Staphylococcus aureus* has got into Daisy's circulation from her nose and spread—it's nothing anyone could have predicted, so please don't blame yourself. The first sign is a crusty area in the nappy area that looks a bit like impetigo, then big red areas form around the crustiness and the skin starts to peel off in big sheets. That's caused by the bacterium, too—it releases a protein that splits off the upper layer of the skin.'

'Is she going to be all right?' Mrs Steward asked, shaking.

'She's definitely in the right place, though I'm going to ring up to the children's ward and get her admitted for a couple of days. Because it's what we call a systemic illness, she might have a bit of a fever and feel a bit unwell.'

'She's been a bit off her food. And cried more than usual, though I thought it was me,' Mrs Steward admitted. 'I've been— No, it doesn't matter.'

'Yes, it does,' Seb said softly. 'You look worried sick. And it's not just this thing with Daisy right now, is it?'

Mrs Steward crumpled. 'It never stops. It's always me looking after her. If she wakes in the night, I have to get up and see to her. If her nappy needs changing, I have to do it. I do all the feeds, all the washing, the house is a mess and my husband's never home. I've tried to keep myself nice but I never have the time and he's just not interested any more. And I think he's having an affair.'

'Hey, I'm sorry.' Seb took her hand and squeezed it. 'Being a parent's a tough job. The toughest job in the world. Nobody's perfect. As long as you do your best, that's good enough.' It was only when you *didn't* do your best that it left scars. He could testify to that.

'But I've only got Daisy. Why's it so hard? My friends have got two or three little ones at home and they're all right. They don't struggle.'

'They probably do,' Seb said. 'It just doesn't feel like it when you're facing a mountain yourself.'

'I'm not going mad.'

'Of course you're not,' he soothed. 'But I think your hormones might not be back to normal yet. So I want you to talk to your health visitor or your family doctor, because I think they can do something to help you.'

Mrs Steward lifted her chin. 'I'm not taking antidepressants. I don't want to be a zombie.'

'There are lots of things besides antidepressants that can help. Talking about your worries is the first step to feeling better,' Seb said. 'And when you're feeling better, you'll enjoy Daisy a lot more, too.'

'She's not going to be taken away from me?' Mrs Steward asked, looking frantic.

'Absolutely not. We'll keep her in for a while,' Alyssa said quietly, 'but that's only because we've got the equipment here that will help us look after her. You can stay with Daisy as long as you like.'

'I'm not going to lose her?'

'You're not going to lose her—to Social Services or anything else,' Seb promised. 'Now, because Daisy's lost some of her skin barrier, she might also be a bit dehydrated.' There was a good chance her electrolyte levels weren't what they should be either. 'What we're going to do is give her something called Ringer's solution, which will rehydrate her. Then we're going to wash these sore areas with saline and put on some emollients to keep her skin moist. We've got some special gel dressings that can help, and she'll be back to normal in a week or so.'

'A *week* or so?' Mrs Steward sounded horrified.

'But you can visit her as often as you like,' Alyssa reiterated, 'and if you want to do some of the care yourself—her feeds and what have you—that'll be fine with the nurses.'

'Will she…well, will she have any scars?' Mrs Steward asked.

'Hopefully not,' Alyssa said. 'But we'll get a plastic surgeon or a dermatologist to give you a specialist view once the infection's cleared up and they can have a proper look at her skin.'

'I just feel as if it's my fault,' Mrs Steward said.

'Not at all. If you were a rubbish mum, you wouldn't have worried about her or brought her in to see us,' Seb said matter-of-factly. 'I know at least half a dozen mums who wouldn't have done as much as you have.' His own being top of the list.

While Alyssa finished treating Daisy, booked the baby onto Paediatrics and paged the plastic surgeon for a visit, Seb extracted a promise from Mrs Steward that she'd see her health visitor.

'Thanks for calming her down for me,' Alyssa said quietly when they left the cubicle.

'No problem.' He smiled. 'It's what I'm here for.'

'I hope she sees her health visitor.'

'Might be worth adding a line or two in your paperwork to the family doctor, asking them to check for postnatal depression in the mum.'

She nodded. 'Good idea. The baby's skin looks pretty bad, though. Do you think it will scar?'

'Not sure,' he admitted. 'But if plastics won't help here, I could have a word with my brother.'

'Your brother?'

'He's a plastic surgeon. I could get her a slot in his clinic at Harley Street.'

Alyssa frowned. 'You're going to recommend private treatment?'

'Yes and no.'

'I don't follow.'

'It's a private clinic, but Charlie blags Theatre time. The clinic can say a baron works there and that impresses all their clients. Meanwhile, he gets free time and medical supplies. He donates his time and treats the patient.'

'And you approve of that?'

He shrugged. 'I don't see a problem. It's a win-win situation. You know what the waiting lists are like, and private medicine isn't cheap. Charlie's just trying to do his bit.'

'Are you telling me in a roundabout way that you do the same thing?'

'I'm not the baron, so I wouldn't get free Theatre time. Anyway, I'm an emergency specialist, not plastics.'

'Right. Well, I won't keep you. Paperwork to do.'

It was a legitimate excuse, but he knew it was an excuse all the same. Alyssa clearly didn't want to spend any more time with him than she had to. Yes, she'd asked for help when she'd known she'd needed it—which was a compliment to his skills, he supposed—but somehow he got the feeling that he'd disappointed her.

He shook himself. It shouldn't matter. It wasn't as if he was in love with her, and apart from the fact he didn't believe in love, what was the point of wanting someone who didn't even like him very much?

Two more patients to see.

And then he'd get his little black book out.

CHAPTER FIVE

'SEB, I can't just put "gorgeous blonde" on the seating plan. I need you to give me a *name*,' Charlie said.

Seb made a bleeping noise. 'Hey, that's my pager. Gotta go.'

'That was the worst impersonation of a bleeper I've ever heard,' Charlie said, laughing. 'And you're not at work anyway. It's half past seven in the evening and you're at home. What's the problem? Can't you choose between the half-dozen women you've got on the go right now?'

'I don't date more than one at a time,' Seb said huffily.

'No, but you've got them lined up,' Charlie said. 'As soon as their date's over and you've taken them to bed, they're crossed off your list and you move on to the next one.'

What was it with people at the moment? Everyone seemed to be criticising his life choices. Well, they suited him just fine. 'Look, I'm the best man. I'm going to be too busy to look after a date, so I'm coming on my own.'

'You're not going to be *that* busy, Seb. All you have to do is pin on a corsage or two, make a speech and read out some cards. And as all the bridesmaids except Vicky are under the age of ten, you'll come out in hives if you do the traditional best man thing of looking after the bridesmaids.'

Seb only heard the phrase 'under the age of ten', and his skin went clammy. 'How many?' he asked through gritted teeth.

'Five. Sophie's cousins.'

Five small girls? Total nightmare. He'd rather have root canal work. Without anaesthetic. 'Uh-huh.'

'Seb, it's OK. We know you're allergic to kids. We're not going to make you look after them. And if you don't want to bring anyone to the wedding, that's fine.'

Though Seb knew his brother well enough to know what Charlie wasn't saying. *But if you don't bring someone, our mother will start lining women up for you.* Seb dated a lot—but he liked to choose his own dates, thank you very much. And he was bored, bored, bored with the debutante type his mother threw at him. He wanted someone more real.

Someone like Alyssa.

He pushed the thought away. He didn't want for ever and ever. He just wanted fun. 'Leave it to me, Charlie.'

'I need to know, Seb. Now.'

'Tomorrow,' Seb promised. 'I'll call you straight after lunch.'

Which gave him a morning to find a date for the wedding. Someone who wouldn't think that, just because he was letting her meet his family, it meant he wanted her to catch the bride's bouquet and drag *him* down the aisle.

Who the hell was he going to ask?

A face floated into his mind. An ordinary face with sea-green eyes and chestnut hair.

Ha. As if *she'd* say yes. She'd already made it clear that she didn't do dates.

Though this wasn't actually a date. It was more a case of helping him out of a jam. So maybe he'd ask her. Tomorrow.

* * *

'This fitness lark definitely isn't what it's cracked up to be,' Lesley Purves said, grimacing. 'I thought it was your legs that were supposed to hurt when you went jogging, not your eyes!'

Alyssa chuckled. 'I've heard of trees jumping out to mug unsuspecting drivers, but not joggers!'

'Danger. Low-flying twig,' Lesley said.

Alyssa was aware that her patient was only joking to stop herself from crying. Lesley had already said her eye felt as if a huge lump of grit was in it, but she couldn't get it out—and it hurt to blink.

'OK, Lesley. What I'm going to do is put a couple of anaesthetic drops in your eye so I can have a look without it hurting you and make sure you've got all the bits of twig out. The chances are you've already done that, but it's probably scraped your cornea, so every time you blink it rubs against the sore bit and it feels as if there's grit there. Then I can put some ointment in, and maybe put a patch over it if it needs it,' Alyssa said.

'Go for it, Doc,' Lesley said. 'And I think next time I'll brave the jeers in the gym rather than sneak out and run in the park where nobody will notice me.'

'Or run wearing sunglasses,' Alyssa suggested.

'Nah, then they'll think I'm a pop star trying to go incognito,' Lesley joked back. 'By the way, who's that gorgeous bloke?'

'What gorgeous bloke?' Alyssa asked, though she already had a good idea of exactly who Lesley meant.

'Tall, dark and drop-dead sexy. Amazing smile. Blue eyes you can't miss, even if you have only got one eye working properly and the other one hurts like crazy,' Lesley said.

'That has to be Seb. Our consultant.'

Lesley sighed. 'Someone that gorgeous has to be spoken for.'

'His girlfriends change more often than the weather,' Alyssa said.

'So I'm in with a chance?' Lesley perked up as Alyssa put the anaesthetic drops in. 'Ooh, I can open my eye now. And it doesn't hurt any more.'

'It will, when the drops wear off,' Alyssa warned. 'Though you can take ibuprofen to help with the pain.'

'Thanks. This will do me for now. So if that fabulous man isn't serious about anyone…I could leave him my phone number,' Lesley mused.

'You *could,* yes. But Seb has this rule: one date and you're out. So it's really not worth making the effort,' Alyssa said.

Seb, who'd been about to twitch the cubicle curtain back and ask Alyssa if she could spare him two seconds, overheard her comment and sighed inwardly. This meant she'd definitely say no. Unless he could persuade her that it wasn't a date. And it wasn't. She would just be saving him from a fate worse than death—Mara and her never-ending list of debutantes.

Though why should Alyssa help him out? She wasn't under any obligation to him. Ah, hell. He'd have to think of something. He'd wait until she'd finished with her patient before he asked her to have lunch with him and discuss a teensy problem he had. And he just had to hope she said yes—to lunch *and* to his proposition.

Alyssa did a full eye examination. Visual acuity was fine. She checked the anterior chamber of the eye with bright light and that seemed OK, too; and there were no foreign bodies in the conjunctival sacs.

'I'm going to put a yellow dye in your eye now,' she told Lesley. 'That'll show me if there's any damage to your cornea.'

She touched a strip of paper impregnated with fluorescein dye into the tear pool of Lesley's eye. 'Blink for me?' she asked.

When Lesley blinked, Alyssa darkened the cubicle and examined Lesley's eye under ultraviolet light. There was a tell-tale stroke of green, where the dye showed up the part of the eye that had been scraped. 'Yep, you've scraped the top of your cornea. I'm going to put something in now that's going to lubricate your eye and make it feel more comfortable—it'll also stop an infection occurring. I think you need a pad on it for day or two, to stop you blinking and making it hurt more.' She put some chloramphenicol ointment into Lesley's eye. 'Can you close your eye for me?' When Lesley had done so, Alyssa folded an eye patch in half and placed it on top of the eye, then placed an unfolded eye patch over it and secured it with micropore tape—that would put enough gentle pressure on the upper lid to stop it opening. 'You're going to need to take this off and replace it three times a day so you can apply some more ointment,' Alyssa said. 'Have you got a friend who can help you?'

'Yes, my flatmate.'

'Good. I'll write you a prescription for the ointment, and I've got a leaflet about eye injuries so your flatmate can see what to do. Once it's healed, I recommend you use the ointment at night for a couple more weeks to make sure it doesn't come back. I'd like you to make an appointment to see your GP in two days' time, so they can check it out for you. But eye injuries heal pretty quickly, so you should be fine,' she said.

'Thanks,' Lesley said as Alyssa handed her the prescription and information leaflet.

'Pleasure.' Alyssa smiled and headed to Reception to see the next patient in the queue.

There was an unexpected rush, which meant she didn't

even get the chance to grab a coffee during the morning. She was about to head off for lunch when she saw Seb coming down the corridor towards her.

'Got a moment?' he asked.

'Um, is it important? I haven't had a break yet since my shift started, and I'm starving.'

Oh, *result*! Even better than he could have anticipated. Seb smiled at her. 'I'm due a break, too. Why don't we have lunch together?'

'Together?'

'Unless you were already meeting someone?' He crossed his fingers behind his back. Please, don't let her be meeting someone.

'No. I was just going to grab a quick sandwich.'

'A sandwich is fine by me.' He gave her his best smile. And, to his relief, it seemed to work, because she nodded.

'So what's the problem?' she asked as they headed for the canteen.

'Sticky one. Mind if we wait until we sit down? I need coffee,' he said.

'Sure.'

He didn't offer to pay for her sandwich—the last thing he wanted to do was put her on the defensive—and he waited until they'd sat down and taken their sandwiches out of their wrappers.

Please, let her say yes.

Please, let her say yes.

Time to put a toe in the water. 'Alyssa, are we friends?'

What kind of a question was that? 'We're colleagues,' she said carefully.

'You trust me at work.'

'Yes.'

'So would you trust me outside work?'

Er—no. He could out-Scott Scott when it came to the charm stakes. 'I'm not sure,' she hedged.

'I'd like to be friends.'

'I'm not sure you're capable of being friends.'

He grinned. That damned dimple again. She just bet he knew about it—and used it to its full effect.

'Of course I'm capable of being friends. I'm friends with Tracey.'

Their charge nurse. Who was happily married with teenage children who were almost grown-up. 'I suppose so,' she admitted.

'So why can't I be friends with you?'

'Because of the sex thing,' she muttered.

He raised an eyebrow. 'We've already agreed we're not going to have sex.'

Her face heated, and she just hoped there weren't any ears flapping nearby. 'Do we have to discuss this *here*?'

Just for a moment, there was a flash of heat in his eyes. Heat that told her he might *say* he didn't want to have sex with her, but he definitely didn't think it. 'OK. I have a proposition for you.'

Uh-oh. This sounded like sex to her.

'I need rescuing.'

She scoffed. 'No way.'

'You won't help me?'

'I didn't say that. Just that you're the last person who needs rescuing.' She took a sip of her coffee. 'You know exactly where you're going and what you want out of life.'

'Which is why I need rescuing.'

She frowned. 'I'm not with you.'

'OK, cards on the table. My brother's getting married next weekend and I'm the best man.'

'And?'

'The best man has to go to the wedding.'

'And you don't want to go?' She understood that. She wasn't over-keen on weddings herself.

'It's not that.'

Knowing Seb, there could only be one reason. 'You want to sleep with the bride?'

'No, I do *not*.'

There was a definite note of anger there. 'You don't like her?' Alyssa guessed.

'Not that either. Sophie's a sweetheart and she's perfect for Charlie—she's a surgeon, too, so she understands him perfectly. No.' He sighed. 'The problem is Mara.'

Alyssa frowned. 'Who's Mara?'

'My mother. She's going to throw debutantes at me. Which would be fine if I was the heir—but I'm not.' He waved a dismissive hand. 'Well, technically, as Charlie's the baron, I suppose I *am* his heir—but, with any luck, I won't be for very much longer. As soon as Charlie and Sophie make me an uncle, that is.' He sighed. 'I just want to go and enjoy my brother's wedding in peace, without my mother spoiling the day with one of her stupid matchmaking schemes.'

So where did she come in to it?

'I need someone to go with me.'

He wanted her to go to a society wedding with him? But why her? He could ask just about any female in the hospital. She raised an eyebrow. 'Seb, why are you asking me? Women will fall over themselves to go with you.'

'And they'll all get the wrong idea.'

'What do you mean?'

'When a man takes you to meet his family, it means he's serious, yes?'

'Well—yes,' she agreed. 'But this is *you* we're talking about. Everyone knows your golden rule. One date, one night of passion and you're on to the next one.'

He winced. Just what Charlie had said. And just what Alyssa herself had said to one of her patients who'd taken a fancy to him that morning. 'Don't make me sound cheap.'

'Seb, you *are* cheap.'

'God, you remind me of Vicky.' At her blank look, he added, 'My baby sister—the brain surgeon.'

'I look like your sister?' Alyssa asked, mystified.

'No. You cut me down in exactly the same way. Actually, maybe asking you to go with me is a bad idea. The pair of you will gang up on me.'

'Why do you want *me* to go with you?'

'Because you'll understand it's not a date, and that meeting my family doesn't mean I'm desperately in love with you until the end of time.'

OK, she could appreciate that. But…a wedding. He wanted her to go to a *wedding*. 'I hate weddings.' They brought back too many bad memories. Like her own wedding. The promise to love, honour and cherish. And Scott had been lying with every single syllable.

'This won't be so bad.' Seb suddenly became animated, as if going in for the hard sell. 'Charlie's managed to get a licence so he can get married at Weston—our family home—and the reception's going to be there, too. If he's got any sense, he'll start using the estate as a wedding venue—it'd stop the estate bleeding him dry.'

'You don't have a very high opinion of people, do you?' Alyssa asked.

'How do you mean?'

'You think all women are gold-diggers, and you look at everything in terms of money.'

He frowned. 'I don't see my work in terms of money. I don't do private medicine.'

She noticed he didn't rebut her comment about gold-diggers. So he *did* think that. 'No, but look at what you've specialised in. Emergency medicine. The patients are in, fixed, and then they're off home or admitted to another ward. You never have to get to know a patient. You can stay detached.'

This was seriously scary. How did she know him so well? Or was he really that shallow, that easy to read? His eyes narrowed. 'Why did you choose emergency medicine, then?'

'Because I like the adrenalin rush.'

'You're an adrenalin junkie?' Oh, welcome to the club. He gave her a lazy grin. 'Wanna drive my car?'

'No.'

'Chicken.'

She grinned back. 'No. You wouldn't be able to handle it.'

'That's a challenge.' He mimed taking off a glove and slapping it onto the table. 'Name the time and place.'

She laughed. 'No, Seb. I admit that you have a fabulous car. Anyone would want to drive it. But you'd fuss the whole time that I wasn't treating your car exactly as you would.'

'Did you do a psychology rotation or something?'

'No. But you said it yourself—what you see is what you get.'

'And you understand that. You don't think there's going to be more. So you know that when I say, "Come to the wedding with me," that's all I mean. I just need someone to accompany me. Not a date. A favour.'

She sighed. 'Thank you for asking me, but no.'

'Why not?'

'I… Look, it's a society wedding.'

'And?'

She looked uncomfortable. 'I'm just ordinary.'

No. Alyssa Ward was very far from ordinary. Not that he was going to admit that to her. Or even to himself. 'You'll be fine. Look, if you're worried about clothes, I'll buy you a posh frock.'

'Thus proving that all women are gold-diggers?'

'No. Thus proving that I'm asking you to do me a favour, so I don't expect you to have to pay for the privilege of saying yes. Think of it as a quid pro quo.' He linked his fingers and leaned back in his chair. 'Hey, we could go shopping together.'

'*What?*'

'We're friends, right? And women like shopping. *Ergo*, as your friend, I'll go shopping with you.'

She laughed.

Result.

'Seb, the only way you'd step into a dress shop is because you fancied the shop assistant.'

He laughed back. 'Are you absolutely sure you haven't done a body swap with my little sister? That's the sort of thing she'd say.' Because she knew him so well.

And so, it seemed, did Alyssa.

He pushed the thought aside. 'Alyssa. Rescue me. Please?'

She sighed. 'Oh, all right. If it'll shut you up.'

'And I mean it about the frock. As a way of saying thank you.'

'I don't need a man to buy me dresses. I can afford my own clothes.'

'I know. But I'd still like to buy you a dress. Think of it as a thank you for saving me.'

She still looked uncomfortable. He sighed. 'OK. What's the real problem?'

'I don't know what you mean.'

'If it's a class thing, forget it. I don't give a damn about class. Neither do my brother and sister. Vic takes people as she finds them, and I should point out that my future sister-in-law has a pronounced East End accent. Soph doesn't have a title. Well, she will have one when she marries Charlie, but she says she's not going to answer to "Lady Sophie". She's a doctor, and that's what counts in her eyes.'

'It's not class.'

So if it wasn't the society thing… 'Because it's a wedding?' he guessed.

'I'm…just not big on weddings.'

His antennae quivered. What had happened to her at a wedding? Had she had to watch the love of her life marrying someone else? 'Neither am I. So come with me. If you really hate it, we can sneak off to the secret garden with a bottle of champagne after I've finished my best man duties.'

'Your family home has a secret garden?'

'Uh-huh. And it's very pretty.'

'How many women have you sneaked out there?'

'Believe me, you don't want to know.' Except none of them had meant anything. Taking Alyssa there, on the other hand… No. He wasn't going to let his thoughts slide in that direction. No strings, no promises, no hassles. And, most definitely, no commitments. He fixed his most charming smile on his face. 'Come with me. We'll have a ball.'

She sighed. 'Why do I get the feeling you're going to nag me until I say yes?'

'Because you understand me, Alyssa. So will you?'

'Do you really think all women are gold-diggers?'

He shrugged. 'In my experience, most of them are.' Starting with the number one woman in his life. Mara. About the only ones he'd met who weren't out for what they could get were his sister and his sister-in-law-to-be.

'In that case,' Alyssa said, 'there's a price for me going with you.'

'As well as the dress?' Seb froze, suddenly realising that he'd thought Alyssa, along with Vicky and Sophie, an exception to his rule. He hadn't thought *she* was a gold-digger. Had he been wrong about her? 'What?'

'A day's pay. Overtime rates for a Saturday night—it *is* a Saturday night, I assume?'

'Yes.' Sick disappointment spread through his stomach. So Alyssa wasn't different after all.

'I think the equipment fund takes cheques.'

He frowned. 'The equipment fund?'

'Mmm-hmm. The one you did the promise auction for? That's my price. Give a day's pay, at overtime rates, to the fund.'

She wanted him to donate the money to charity?

So he *hadn't* got her wrong.

He smiled. 'Done.'

CHAPTER SIX

ALYSSA refused to let Seb go shopping with her—or pay for her outfit. She also refused flatly to tell him what her outfit looked like. Even more annoyingly, she insisted on buying her own present for Charlie and Sophie, and she didn't tell him what *that* was either. And the clerk of the department store that held the wedding list refused to tell him, even when he laid on the charm and explained that he was the best man and therefore he needed to know.

Women!

But when Seb parked his car outside Alyssa's flat on the Saturday morning and she answered the door, he did a double-take.

This was Alyssa, the quiet but efficient registrar in ED who had an acid tongue if you got on the wrong side of her, and who always wore professional-looking black trousers and a cream shirt at work? He'd seen her wearing a little black dress on their prize night out, but that hadn't prepared him at all for the way she looked right at that moment.

Alyssa Ward, off duty, in a floaty summery dress and high heels. The dress was a dark aqua and brought out the sea green of her eyes. And it was made of some gauzy fabric that had Seb looking twice at the skirt to see if he could catch a glimpse of her legs. No hat, but her hair looked shiny and glossy and he itched to touch it. As usual, she wore little make-up—but what she wore was enough to emphasise the curve of her mouth and the size of her eyes.

If he told her how amazing she looked, she wouldn't believe him. She'd think he was just laying on the charm. And he didn't want her to think he was being insincere. So he simply smiled and said, 'You scrub up very nicely, Dr Ward.'

'So do you, Mr Radley.' She locked the door behind her. 'Do I take it there's a top hat and tailcoat that goes with that outfit?'

The waistcoat, cravat, wing-tip white shirt and black dress trousers. He nodded. 'Though they're not comfortable to drive in, and I don't want to crease the coat. They're in the back of the car.' He smiled at her. 'Want to drive?'

'No.'

'Don't say I didn't offer.' He opened the passenger door for her.

'I feel as if I should be wearing a hat and gloves,' she said as she climbed in.

'No, you're fine as you are.' More than fine. Maybe it had been a bad idea to ask Alyssa to go to the wedding with him. He'd thought she was safe. That they were colleagues, and on the cusp of being friends. He liked her.

Being attracted to her was something else entirely. If he was stupid enough to make a pass at her, it'd ruin their relationship for ever. And was it worth it, for just one night? No. He could control himself. And he knew what he had to do. Drive to Weston, spike Mara's guns by introducing Alyssa to her, do his best man duties, dance with Alyssa a couple of times and then drive her home.

Easy.

* * *

Alyssa enjoyed the drive down to Weston. Seb was a good driver, and a rummage in the glove box showed her that his taste in music was similar to hers. And he had a good singing voice—he wasn't embarrassed to sing along with the chorus of his favourite tracks, and she found herself joining him.

But the house itself…was intimidating. A huge old pile. Somewhere she really didn't belong, except maybe as a tourist. 'It's a stately home,' she whispered as Seb guided the car down the incredibly long tree-lined drive.

'Yes.' He seemed completely unconcerned.

She supposed it was because he'd grown up there. Even so. 'I wasn't expecting it to be this *big*.'

'It's also cold, damp, has a roof that eats money and contains a dra—' He stopped.

'A dragon?' Alyssa queried.

'Oh, hell.' He sighed. 'Just kick my ankle if you hear me start to come out with anything like that, will you? I'm supposed to be on my best behaviour today. For Charlie's sake.'

'So who's the dragon?'

'My dear mama.' He rolled his eyes. 'Oh, she'll be perfectly nice to you, don't worry.'

'But you clash with her.' It wasn't a question. His expression told her just how much he disliked his mother. What had Mara done to him? Alyssa wondered. And was Mara the reason he never dated a woman more than once—in case she turned out to be like his mother?

'I usually manage to avoid her. Except today obviously I can't.' He shrugged. 'I told you I needed rescuing.'

'Should've brought my white charger and my lance,' Alyssa said lightly. 'Hey. You'll be fine.'

'Uh-huh. Just as well I'm good at fake smiles.' Seb took a

deep breath as he parked the car. 'Come and meet the troops. Once the introductions are over, I should be able to keep us away from Mama Dearest and Barry.'

'Barry being…?'

'Her husband.'

Not 'my stepfather', she noticed. Not a good relationship there either. Which went a long way to explaining why Seb was the way he was—smiling and charming and perfectly polite, but never letting anyone close to him. How long had Mara been married to Barry? she wondered. And Seb was clearly the middle child—Charlie, being the baron, had to be the eldest, and Seb had referred to Vicky as his 'baby sister'. Had Seb had too little of everyone's attention when he'd been young?

'Is he that bad?' she asked.

'Put it this way, you're supposed to kiss a frog and he turns into a handsome prince. Mara clearly got her spell the wrong way round.'

So his mother was a witch and his stepfather was a toad? Ouch. She wished she hadn't asked. 'Hey. Your cravat's crooked,' she said when he'd shrugged his tailcoat on. 'Let me.' Except adjusting his cravat meant her fingers touched his skin. Just once—but it felt as if she'd had a small static shock.

Their gazes met and held for a moment, and she stepped back before she gave into the temptation to reach up and kiss him. Stupid. This wasn't a date. This was helping him out of a hole.

He held his arm out to her and she slipped her fingers through the crook of his elbow. The house loomed in front of them, and Alyssa wished she'd let Seb go shopping with her. At least he could have told her if she was dressed up enough. Right now, she didn't feel as if she'd pass muster. Not at a society wedding. She looked too plain and ordinary. She wasn't going to fit in at all.

'Relax. We're not going to the scaffold,' he said out of the corner of his mouth.

It just felt like it.

And then they were inside. A dark-haired, blue-eyed woman who bore a resemblance to Seb came towards them.

'Sebastian.' She held out a cheek to be kissed.

Alyssa, seeing him hesitate, kicked his ankle.

He switched on the charm. 'Mama, dearest.'

Alyssa had heard him say that before, and every time it had been dripping in sarcasm. This time, it sounded full of *bonhomie*. Clearly Seb was a practised liar. And she'd had enough of practised liars to last her a lifetime.

'Let me introduce you to Alyssa. Alyssa, this is my mother, Mara.'

Mara gave her a thin smile and held her hand out. 'Pleased to meet you, Alyssa.'

Alyssa was about to return the politeness when it struck her. She knew nothing about etiquette. What did she call Mara? Obviously not Mrs Radley, because she'd been a baroness. And Seb's father had been a baron, so Mara had clearly been Lady Mara at one point—but since she'd remarried, would that make her a plain Mrs? And what was her surname anyway? Hoping it was the right thing to do, she smiled back and took Mara's hand. 'You too, Lady Mara.'

'And this is Barry, my mother's husband.'

One glance, and Alyssa had to hold in a nervous giggle. Barry *did* look like a toad. Swarthy skin, greasy hair, shorter than she was and quite broad. On Seb, the tailcoat looked elegant and sexy—he could have been a Regency dandy. But on Barry the tailcoat looked grotesque and out of proportion. She just wished that Seb hadn't put that picture of a toad in her mind. She could imagine Barry behind the wheel of Seb's car, delightedly calling, 'Poop, Poop!' like Mr Toad in *Wind in the Willows.*

'Pleased to meet you,' she said, hoping that her smile looked genuine.

'Where's Charlie?' Seb asked.

'Wandering about somewhere with Vicky.'

'I need to make some more introductions. Come on, Alyssa.' Seb took her hand and tugged her away with him.

'Seb, that was rude,' she said quietly.

'I can't stand being in the same room as them. They're a pair of bloodsuckers,' Seb said vehemently. 'Dad made Charlie promise he'd look after our mother when he died. When she remarried, that should have released him from the promise. But, no, not Charlie. He's such an idiot. He lets them live here as if *they* were the baron and his lady, and he picks up the tab. He says it's his duty.'

She couldn't think of anything to say, so she took the wise option and kept her mouth closed.

'And, of course, Mama Dearest won't dream of helping him by opening the house to the public or holding weddings here or something—anything to make the house work for part of its keep. Old houses like this cost a fortune in maintenance, and you wouldn't believe the regulations when it comes to doing any work on the place. And she tries to interfere in the way Charlie's manager runs the estate—even though she doesn't have the first clue about finances or estate management. All that woman knows how to do is *spend*.' His mouth was set in a thin line.

So that was the root of Seb's gold-digger fixation. But now wasn't the time to talk about it. 'Seb, we're at a wedding right now,' she reminded him. 'And you're the best man. Do I have to kick your ankle again?'

'No.' He tightened his fingers round hers. 'Thank you for that. I told you I needed rescuing.'

And he'd been telling the truth. Her heart went out to him. Though she could see another shadow in his face—a shadow she could at least put to flight. 'Hey. I'm not going to breathe a word of your private business to anyone at the hospital, before you ask.'

'I know. I trust you.'

Then he looked at her in utter shock. Alyssa guessed that he'd never said those words to anyone female before. Except, maybe, the sister she reminded him of. The sister he was just about to introduce her to.

He dropped her hand. 'Let's go and find the wedding party.'

Charlie was a slightly taller, broader and softer version of Seb—he wasn't quite so polished—and Alyssa liked him on sight. She also liked Vicky, who had the same slate-blue eyes and dark hair as Seb, the same slightly mischievous feel about her, and who said exactly what she thought.

'About time you turned up, Seb. I've been doing your best man's duties all morning,' she said.

'Oh, rubbish. I've done everything I was supposed to,' Seb said.

'What about looking after the bridesmaids?' Vicky pointed out.

Seb rolled his eyes. 'I've already discussed *that* with the groom. The deal is, I'll look after you, as chief bridesmaid— but not the tribe.' He turned to Alyssa. 'She seriously thinks I'll look after five girls under the age of ten?'

'What is it with you and kids, Seb?' Alyssa asked.

He scowled. 'I'm allergic to them.'

'No, you're not. You're just hopeless with them and you don't like it because they—unlike their mothers—can resist your charm.' Vicky winked at him. 'Go and do best man things and I'll take Alyssa to meet Soph. You can't come because it's bad luck.'

'It's bad luck for the *groom* to see the bride before the wedding, not the best man,' Seb corrected her.

Vicky snorted. 'For someone who's allergic to weddings, too, you know a lot, don't you?'

'Of course. He's an encyclopaedia. The fount of all knowledge,' Alyssa said.

'Oh, that's it,' Seb said in disgust. 'I *knew* you'd gang up on me if I introduced you to each other.'

'Because you deserve it,' Charlie said, laughing. 'Wait till Soph comes down.'

'Yeah, I know. She'll join them,' Seb said glumly. 'Women! Well, as best man, my duty is to pour the condemned man a last malt whisky.'

'You mean, *you* want one.' Charlie clapped his brother on the back. 'Come on, then. Let's sneak off to the library. You know where we are if you need us, Vicky.'

Vicky gave them an amused glance, tucked her hand into the crook of Alyssa's arm and led her up the sweeping staircase.

'I think Tracey's right—you are a match for Seb,' Vicky said with a grin.

'You discussed me with Tracey? As in Tracey Fry?' Alyssa's eyes narrowed. 'So that raffle draw *was* a fix, then.'

'Um…' Vicky coughed. 'I'm sorry. We were trying to do the right…' She stopped. 'We thought you might, um, be good for each other. But if we got it wrong, I apologise unreservedly. I know my brother can be a louse towards women.' She gave Alyssa a curious look. 'So what's the deal between you? The last thing Seb told me, he was coming on his own.'

'I don't want to betray Seb's confidence,' Alyssa said carefully.

'Let me guess. He realised that if he turned up solo, Mama Dearest would start throwing debs at him and he'd end up having his usual fight with her, and he didn't want Charlie's day ruined.'

Alyssa felt her eyes widen. 'No comment.'

'I thought as much. He's probably right,' Vicky said.

'I did notice a bit of tension between them,' Alyssa said carefully. And very little warmth either.

'That woman has a lot to answer for,' Vicky said dryly. But she refused to be drawn further. She simply said, 'I'm glad Seb has a proper female friend at last.'

'I'm not his girlfriend,' Alyssa said quickly.

'No, I mean a *friend*—someone who can show him that not all women are the same. He's always been bad, but he got worse after Julia.'

'Julia's his ex?'

Vicky shook her head. 'No, Charlie's—but she was seeing someone else. Charlie walked in on them together, the week before they were supposed to get married.'

Ouch. No wonder Seb had seemed so angry when Alyssa had suggested that he wanted to sleep with the bride. He'd already seen the brother he loved hurt that way once. And as for Charlie discovering his fiancée had been cheating... Alyssa could identify with that. Except, in her case, it hadn't been before the wedding. And it had been a little more complicated than just cheating.

'Seb was murderous. And even though we both love Sophie, he's still... Oh.' Vicky shook her head. 'I think you're bright enough to work him out for yourself. The real Seb Radley, I mean, not the playboy he makes everyone think he is.' She smiled. 'But, hey, it's Charlie and Sophie's wedding day. Don't listen to me moaning.'

'You just love your brother and want to see him happy,' Alyssa said quietly.

If only she'd had a sibling who'd looked out for her, like Seb's brother and sister. Someone who would have stopped her making a fool out of herself over Scott. Then again, Alyssa had ignored her mother's doubts. So maybe she'd just had to find out for herself. The hard way.

When Vicky introduced Alyssa to Sophie, Alyssa liked the bride on sight, too. Bubbly, blonde and bouncy—and her room was filled with people. A woman who was obviously Sophie's mother, fussing around her hair. And five small bridesmaids, complete with their mothers who were making last-minute adjustments to hair, explaining that, no, they couldn't wear lipstick or sparkly nail varnish and—to the youngest two—yes, they'd have a special teddy to carry, a teddy who wore a special dress like Aunty Sophie.

Kisses and hugs and laughs and smiles. So this was what a big, noisy family was like. Everything Alyssa had dreamed about when she'd been a kid—and had felt guilty about wishing for something she couldn't have.

And how different this was from her own, so very quiet, wedding day.

'Excuse the bedlam,' Sophie said with a grin.

'It's OK. I like kids,' Alyssa said.

'Unlike my future brother-in-law.'

'Think of me as his temporary stand-in. I've worked in emergency medicine for a long time, so I have tricks up my sleeve,' Alyssa said with a grin. She cast a glance at the youngest bridesmaids. 'Does anyone want to hear a princess story?'

Four young heads turned her way—and then a fifth, slightly older one, who was clearly trying to look cool and grown-up but also wanted to hear the story. There was a chorus of 'ooh' and 'yes, please' and 'wicked'—all at the same time.

Alyssa smiled. 'Right. The rules are, you have to stay put and sit very, very still, so your mums can finish doing your hair. And I'll tell you the story of a very, very special princess…'

'I think,' Sophie said to Vicky, *sotto voce*, 'we've just found the woman who can make Seb into a real human being.'

'It's getting *them* to see that. They both say they're just friends.'

'That's a step up from the norm, where Seb's concerned.' Sophie smiled. 'And, hey, it's my wedding day. A day when dreams can come true.'

Vicky grinned back. 'Just don't lob your flowers at them. I don't think the direct approach will work with those two somehow.'

'Pity. I suppose locking them in a dungeon until they agree to get married wouldn't work either?'

'There aren't any dungeons at Weston,' Vicky said.

Sophie's eyes gleamed. 'We could arrange it…'

At last, the bridesmaids were ready.

Vicky looked at her watch. 'Time to go. Unless you want to keep Charlie waiting a few minutes, Soph?'

Sophie shook her head. 'I haven't seen him since last night, thanks to you lot being so superstitious.'

'It's bad luck to see the groom before the wedding,' Vicky and Fran, Sophie's mother, chorused.

'I know. And I can't hold out any longer.' She turned to Alyssa with a pleading look. 'Vicky wouldn't even let me talk to him on my mobile phone this morning.'

'Uh-oh. Mushiness alert,' Vicky said with a grin. 'Ready to do our princessy bit behind Aunty Sophie, kids?'

There was a chorus of 'Yes' and they trooped down the stairs together.

Sophie was the epitome of a bride. Radiant, beautiful, wearing a truly stunning dress and a very simple veil and headdress, and carrying a simple sheaf of Calla lilies.

Alyssa pushed the little pangs of envy aside. Marriage hadn't worked out for her, but it didn't mean it wouldn't work out for other people. She followed the others down the stairs and into the hall where Charlie and Sophie were getting married. Seb was standing at the front, next to Charlie. Alyssa was about to slip into a seat at the back on the groom's side when Seb caught her eye and motioned to the front.

He'd saved her a seat next to him? Her eyes widened. She wasn't officially part of the family. She'd been a last-minute invitee, too. Piggybacking on Seb's invite, really. She didn't belong there.

'Please,' he mouthed.

Well, she was supposed to be there as a buffer. She couldn't be much use to him if she was sitting halfway across the room. She nodded and made her way to the front, sliding in next to Mara.

The ceremony began, and as the registrar spoke the so-familiar words, she found herself reliving another wedding, five years before. A wedding where she'd made her vows so earnestly, believing every single word—and all the time, Scott's vows had been false. Every word a lie.

She realised Seb had taken his place beside her when a hand curled round hers and squeezed it briefly before letting it go again. Hell, it must show on her face that she found this hard. Or maybe Seb remembered she'd told him she didn't like weddings.

She was almost tempted to tell him why. He'd keep it to himself, she knew that. But what was the point in stirring up memories that were better forgotten?

And then Sophie and Charlie were pronounced husband and wife. Charlie kissed his bride. And confetti flew in all directions.

CHAPTER SEVEN

ALYSSA kept the bridesmaids entertained during the interminable photo sessions with stories and songs, then Sophie's mother joined her.

'You're really good with kids,' Fran said approvingly. 'Come from a big family, do you, love?'

'No, there's just me and my mum. But I see a lot of kids at the hospital and I'm used to telling them stories to get them to lie still so I can examine them,' Alyssa explained.

'So you're a doctor, like my Soph. Are you a surgeon, too?'

'No, I'm in the emergency department,' Alyssa said.

Fran gave her a sidelong look. 'You know, you're not what I expected Seb's girlfriend to be like. I thought you'd be snooty and stick-thin, and turn your nose up at anything more than a lettuce leaf.'

Alyssa chuckled. 'Apart from the fact I'm not Seb's girlfriend, I like my food—especially puddings—and I was terrified about coming here today because it's a society wedding and I thought I'd feel a bit out of place.'

'It's a *family* wedding,' Fran corrected her. 'Our side isn't blue-blooded.' Not that she seemed bothered by it, because she added with a smile, 'Everyone's going to mix in fine. But you are here with Seb, aren't you, love?'

'Yes. Though he's my colleague, not my partner.'

'Hmm. Well, I hope he treats his patients better than he treats other people,' Fran said.

'He's an excellent doctor.'

'Soph says he's got a heart of gold under all that party-party-party front.' But Fran didn't look quite so sure.

'She's right. There's more to him than meets the eye,' Alyssa said, and expertly steered the conversation back to Sophie and Charlie and how happy they looked. She really didn't want to discuss Seb behind his back. And it felt strange, standing up for him, even though Fran was making exactly the same points Alyssa herself had thought about Seb.

Anyway, Seb didn't need anyone to stand up for him. He could fight his own battles.

Then it was time for the meal. Seb had everyone eating out of his hand and laughing along with his jokes during the best man's speech, and Alyssa caught a glance of the real Seb when he made the toasts. 'To the bride and groom. And may life be always good to them.' For someone who didn't believe in love, Seb was absolutely sincere. He really did want things to turn out right for Sophie and Charlie.

He even managed to overcome his dislike of children long enough to compliment all the bridesmaids, to the point where their mums were all pink and glowing with pride. And then he caught Alyssa's eye and raised his glass in a silent toast to her.

Thanks for helping him through this and keeping the kids away from him, she guessed.

Though, weirdly, it felt more personal than that. Special. Almost as if he were toasting her as his bride…

Oh, no. It must be the wedding atmosphere getting to her. Because she wasn't going to be anyone's bride ever again. And Seb definitely wasn't going to get married. He'd told her that explicitly. *My partners understand the situation right from the start. I'm not going to get married, or live with someone, or have a permanent relationship of any kind.*

Which was fine by her. They understood each other perfectly.

At the reception, Sophie and Charlie had the first dance, followed by Seb and Vicky, as best man and chief bridesmaid. Alyssa was more than happy to watch from the sidelines. Then Seb came over to her, tugged her to her feet, casually looped his arm round her shoulders and kept her with him as they circulated, glass of champagne in hand.

Alyssa found some of the guests a bit toffee-nosed and shallow, but she noticed that Sophie's family weren't the least bit fazed by it and persuaded everyone to join in the dancing. Even Mara seemed to unbend a little.

How very different from Alyssa's own small wedding. She'd only had her mum there to represent her family. Scott's family—well, he'd said that he was on bad terms with them, hadn't spoken to them for years. So they'd just had a few friends there.

But, in the circumstances, it was no wonder that Scott had wanted a small wedding.

'Hey. Are you all right?' Seb asked.

She shook herself. 'I'm fine.'

'You looked a bit sad just then.'

'Weddings do that to me,' she said lightly.

'Want to grab some champagne and escape to the secret garden?'

She shook her head. 'Seb, you're the best man. You're supposed to stay visible.'

He sighed. 'Dance with me, then. Before I get dragged into dancing with all the bridesmaids.'

'They're lovely kids, Seb. You'd have fun dancing with them—and they'd feel like princesses, with you dressed like that.' And looking so handsome—though she wasn't going to tell him that. She was sure he already knew it anyway.

'Kids and I don't mix,' he said firmly.

She gave up trying to persuade him, and put her glass on a nearby table.

Seb, as Alyssa had expected, was an excellent dancer, and had her spinning round effortlessly. She was enjoying herself thoroughly when the beat changed.

A slow dance.

Well, bang went that one, then. Seb had probably already spotted his next conquest among the wedding guests, and would start his seduction with a snatched slow dance.

But, to Alyssa's surprise, Seb pulled her into his arms.

Slow dancing with Seb Radley. Hmm. She felt as if she were floating on air. But she'd only drunk two glasses of champagne—her glass, still sitting on the table, was full. Must be vintage champagne, then. Extra bubbles. And they'd gone to her head. Why else would she feel like this?

As they moved round the dance floor, she realised that Seb's hands weren't where they should be.

'Seb,' she hissed in his ear.

'Mmm?'

'Your hands are on my bottom.'

'I know.' His breath caressed her ear, sending a shiver down her spine. 'Yours are round my neck. It's called dancing. It's what people do at a wedding reception.'

Yes, but there was dancing and there was *dancing*. And the way Seb was touching her didn't count as just dancing. It was much more intimate than that. Promising. Tantalising.

'You just stroked me,' she accused.

'Sorry.'

He didn't look or sound repentant, though. He looked like…well, like a pirate, she thought as she squinted at him. Dark and dangerous.

Must be the champagne making her think like that.

Right at that moment she didn't care. He was temptation personified. And she was ready to fall. 'Seb?' she whispered.

'Mmm?'

She reached up and touched her lips to his.

Oh-h. His mouth was soft. Gentle. Promising. And she wanted more.

She kissed him again, nibbling at his lower lip.

And then he opened his mouth against hers and turned the kiss straight up to fever pitch. She couldn't remember anyone kissing her this well before—even Scott. All she could think of was the way Seb's mouth moved on hers. The slow, teasing persuasion of his tongue. Inciting. Daring her to take it further. Promising her delights—more, more and still more.

Everything she wanted.

Everything she'd dreamed of.

All she had to do was take it—take *him*.

And then he stopped.

'Why?' she whispered.

'Because we're in the middle of the dance floor, there are lots of people watching us—oh, and a photographer or two,' he whispered back. 'If you really want pages from the gossip rags pinned up in our staffroom with our picture circled on it and captions written beside it…'

'No-o.' Definitely not. So stopping what they were doing was the sensible thing to do. He was absolutely right.

He kissed her earlobe. 'And you've had too much champagne. You don't know what you're doing.'

Oh, yes, she did. 'I'm over the age of consent,' she reminded him. '*Well* over.'

He chuckled. 'Don't make yourself sound like a dried-up old prune. You can't be more than thirty.'

'Thirty exactly.'

'Which makes you a baby. Two years younger than me.' He dropped a kiss on the sensitive spot just beneath her ear. 'I want to, Alyssa. Believe me, I want to make love with you. All night. Beneath the stars in the secret garden. You, me, a bottle of champagne—and I promise you, you wouldn't feel the cold. There'd be too much heat between us.' He pulled her just that little bit closer, so she could feel the evidence of his arousal pressing against her. 'But you'd hate me in the morning. And I respect you too much.'

Before Alyssa could argue, someone tapped on her shoulder. 'Swap partners?' the woman asked.

'Sure,' Seb said easily.

And then he was dancing with someone else. Tall, blonde and beautiful. Just his type. Alyssa tried to damp down the throb of jealousy and concentrate on chatting to her new dancing partner. And the next, and the next. Seb was moving from woman to woman. Mr No Commitment was definitely making his point. One dance, and that was it.

Well, what had she expected?

This wasn't a date anyway, she reminded herself.

She accepted another glass of champagne, hoping that the bubbles would restore her lift. Though they didn't. Nothing did, until she found herself back in Seb's arms again.

'On your second round of the room, are you?' she asked.

'No.' He grinned at her. 'But Barry was heading in your direction. Your feet will thank me for this tomorrow.'

'Why?' she asked, mystified.

'Because, apart from the fact that his face would be right in your cleavage, he can't dance. At all.' He spun her in a circle, and pulled her back into his arms. 'And I'd hate you to have bruised toes and still be hobbling around at work on Monday.'

There wasn't much she could say to that.

And then the tempo changed again. Another slow dance. Was he going to step away again?

But he didn't. And right now it felt as if there was nobody else in the room except the two of them. She snuggled against him. 'Mmm. Know what? I could curl up and go to sleep right now in your arms.'

Oh, hell. This wasn't supposed to happen. She'd been here to rescue him and stop his mother throwing air-headed posh girls at him. And to stop him telling his mother what he thought of her. Alyssa had been supposed to keep him in line.

How on earth could he stay in line when she was here in his arms, like this? He wanted her. Badly. He was having a tough time not dragging her off into the nearest quiet room, locking the door and making love with her. The way she'd kissed him, earlier…

But it was just the effect of the champagne. The waiters were skilled at topping up the guests' glasses without them realising, and that made it impossible to tell how much you'd drunk. Which was why Seb—both as the best man and as the one who was driving them home—had stuck to one very small glass of malt whisky before the wedding and one glass of champagne with the meal, which he hadn't allowed the waiters to top up, and had drunk mineral water ever since. He was perfectly sober.

But Alyssa had kissed him. Lord, how she'd kissed him.

That was *definitely* champagne-induced—she didn't date, much less anything else.

Even the memory of that kiss made him hard. And made him want to do it again. Preferably without an audience and without any barriers of clothing between them.

Ah, hell. Maybe he should take her home now. On the other hand, it was a long drive back to London. And neither of them was on duty tomorrow. It wouldn't matter if they stayed the night.

In his room.

Except he'd do the honourable thing and sleep in a chair. He could take advantage of her, yes, but she'd never forgive him for it when she was sober again. Besides, when he made love with Alyssa—and he knew now it was a when, not an if— he wanted her to be stone cold sober. And drunk only on him.

'You're tired, sweetheart?'

'Mmm.'

'Come on.'

'We're going home?'

'We're going to have a nap,' he corrected.

She snuggled closer. 'You're going to stay with me?'

'Yes.' Though he'd make sure there was at least two arms' length of space between them until she'd fallen asleep, and then he'd move straight to a chair. His self-control wasn't that good. If she was naked and in his arms, he'd make love with her. No question about it.

The champagne had definitely gone to her head, because she stumbled on the stairs. He didn't want her to fall. So that was the only reason he picked her up and carried her up the rest of the stairs. To his room. And locked the door behind them.

Gently, he set her down on the bed, switched on the bedside light, drew the curtains and snapped off the overhead light.

By the time he'd done that, Alyssa was asleep.

Which was just as well, for his peace of mind. Though she looked so cute, like a little dormouse, tousled and... His smile faded. The floaty material of her dress was going to crease like mad. She'd be so embarrassed tomorrow morning if she had to walk out of here wearing the clothes she'd obviously slept in.

There was only one thing for it.

He nudged her shoulder, very gently. 'I need to undress you, sleepyhead,' he said softly.

'Mmm.'

Gently, he manoeuvred her over to her side, unzipped her dress and eased her out of it.

Oh, Lord. Curves. What curves. He hadn't even guessed that her work clothes hid curves this good. Her bra was a confection of aqua-coloured lace, her knickers matched, and she was wearing hold-up stockings. She looked absolutely mouthwatering, and he itched to strip away the lace. Strip away everything so they were skin to skin. Then cover every single centimetre of her body with his hands and his mouth. Explore her.

This was a woman he wanted to kiss all over. Right here. Right now. No barriers. Find out where her sensitive spots were. Where she liked being touched. Licked. Sucked.

He had to tear his gaze away. She was too tempting. Much, much too tempting. He could only do this if he didn't look at her.

He kept his back to her while he removed her shoes. She had such pretty feet. Nice ankles. He couldn't help sliding the tips of his fingers into the hollow below her anklebone. It would be so easy, so easy, to let his hands drift further up her leg and—

No.

He moved away while he still had the strength to do it, and took off his tailcoat. His waistcoat and cravat followed. He kicked off his shoes and put his wallet on the cabinet next to his bed, then padded into the *en suite* bathroom to clean his teeth and splash his face with cold water. What he really needed right now was a cold shower, but the noise of the water might wake Alyssa. And he couldn't face any recriminations. The morning would be better.

When he was sure he was under control again, he went back into the bedroom. He'd be fine, sleeping in a chair. But he needed to get Alyssa under the duvet, or she'd wake in the night, freezing.

He put her dress on a hanger, then shifted the duvet and rolled Alyssa onto the mattress. He was about to settle the duvet round her when she murmured drowsily, 'I want a cuddle.'

Oh, no. Bad idea.

Trying to ignore the demands of his body, he tucked the duvet round her.

'Seb. Please?' she whispered.

Ah, hell. How could he resist?

It took him seconds to get rid of his shirt, trousers and socks. He slid into bed beside her, switched off the bedside light and curled his body round hers, pulling her back against him.

'Mmm.' She snuggled back against him and within moments her breathing had become deeper, more even. She was asleep.

He touched his mouth to her bare shoulder. 'Ah, Alyssa. If you had any idea how self-sacrificing I've been…' But no. She trusted him. He wasn't going to break that trust. Even though every nerve in his body was screaming at him to lose himself within her.

* * *

Some time later, Seb woke to find Alyssa's hand exploring his body.

Talk about testing his self-control. If she kept this up, he'd either be in line for a sainthood or he'd snap completely.

And he had a feeling it was going to be the latter. Especially if her hand started moving south.

He caught her hand and gently moved it away from his chest. 'Alyssa. Go to sleep.'

'Mmm, Seb. You feel nice.'

He wished he'd left her hand where it had been. Because now it was her mouth touching his skin instead. Drawing a line of kisses along his collar-bone.

He couldn't remember the last time a woman had seduced him. And he definitely couldn't remember the last time a woman had seduced him this well.

'Alyssa, if you don't stop,' he warned, 'I can't guarantee my self-control's going to hold out.'

'Is that right?' Her voice was a throaty, husky murmur. Full of mischief and laughter.

'Do you know what you're doing?' he asked.

And then he stopped thinking as her other hand came into play, brushing down over his abdomen, and slid under the edge of his jockey shorts and curled itself around his erection. His breath hissed. 'Alyssa.'

'Mmm. Nice. *Very* nice,' she purred. 'Make love with me, Seb.'

He almost heard the explosion as his control snapped. One second later, Seb was flat on his back and he'd pulled Alyssa on top of him. Oh, yes. Bliss. The only thing between their bodies was the lace of her knickers. He could feel the heat of her sex through the thin barrier—and it was too much for him.

He sat up, keeping her on his lap, and kissed her. Hard. He slid his fingers through her hair—so soft, so silky—and anchored her mouth to his. Kissed her as if the world was going to end in four seconds' time.

With his other hand, he unsnapped the clasp of her bra and gently removed the garment. Lord, her breasts felt good against his skin. The hard tips of her nipples brushed against his chest, making him groan. He pushed up against her, wanting her. Wanting her so badly he almost forgot something important.

Almost, but not quite.

He broke the kiss. 'Alyssa. Are you quite sure about this?'

'Yes. I want you, Seb. I want to make love with you. I want to feel you inside me.'

Oh, Lord, yes. Now, now, *now*. He could hardly breathe. 'Give me a moment.' Just long enough to reach for his wallet. He wanted to turn the light on, see what he was doing. See *Alyssa*. But the light might shock her out of this mood, might make her change his mind. He was too far gone to cope with that. Especially when she was wriggling on his lap like that, rubbing her sex against his.

Wallet. Condom. Open packet. His hands were shaking so badly, he could hardly put the damned thing on. But at last he managed it.

'Alyssa.' He lifted her slightly, moved the material of her knickers to one side, and fitted the tip of his penis to her entrance.

Please, don't let him be dreaming.

Or, if he was, please, don't let him wake up. Not yet.

He took a shuddering breath as she eased down on him. 'Oh, *yes*.'

'Seb,' she whispered, and he was lost. He tilted his hips, pushing as hard as he could into her. She met him kiss for kiss, thrust for thrust.

This was like nothing he could ever remember. Alyssa blew his mind.

Which in itself was dangerous. It made him want more. More than just tonight. Ah, hell. He couldn't do this. Shouldn't do this. Relationships weren't for him. He liked the thrill of the chase. He didn't want to settle down, become boring, see his relationship grow stale and fall apart. It wasn't going to happen. He and Alyssa weren't really compatible. He wasn't compatible with anyone; he was a lone wolf, and he liked it that way.

His hands cupped Alyssa's breasts. She felt perfect. The absolutely perfect shape and weight for his hands. He couldn't help rubbing his thumbs against her nipples. She hissed in pleasure, arching back, and he took advantage of the position to kiss her throat. He could feel her pulse against his mouth; her heart was beating as fast as his own. Pulsing with the same burning need, the same desire.

His head dipped lower and he took one nipple into his mouth, drawing hard on it. She shuddered and threaded her fingers through his hair, her fingertips massaging his scalp and urging him on. 'Yes,' she breathed.

He released her nipple and blew on her damp skin, making her shudder, then teased her other breast in exactly the same way. Just when she was quivering, he shifted and rolled her onto her back, still staying inside her. She wrapped her legs round his waist, pulling him closer, and he groaned her name.

He'd never lost himself so completely with someone. Right now, he could barely remember his own name—all he was aware of was Alyssa. The way she made him feel. Her warm, sweet depths surrounding him. Her mouth opening under his. The fast, desperate thrum of his blood through his veins—the

pace matched exactly by hers. Two hearts beating as one.
Two bodies moving as one.

And then the splintering as the stars exploded in his head.

CHAPTER EIGHT

ALYSSA woke with a dry mouth and a head that definitely had a woodpecker inside it, trying to drill its way out. She would have moved, except her pillow was soft and comfortable.

And hairy.

She opened one eye, and managed to focus for just long enough to confirm her suspicions. She was sprawled all over a male body. A naked male body. A body belonging to the Honourable Sebastian Radley.

Not good. She remembered dancing with him last night. Kissing him, too. But she hadn't drunk *that* much champagne, had she? Surely not enough to spend the night with Seb.

More memories returned to heat her skin. Oh, no. After all she'd promised herself, she'd ended up being yet another notch in his bedpost.

A very pleasurable notch, admittedly. Seb had had enough practice to be very good indeed at making love. He was skilled enough to know exactly where she'd enjoy being touched, being kissed, being stroked. He'd given her an orgasm that had left her whole body fizzing.

But she also knew Seb's rule: immediate curtailment of relationship after sex. Which meant everything between them stopped, as of now.

Not that they'd *had* a relationship exactly.

'Welcome back to the land of the living, honey,' he whispered.

Oh, no. This was even worse. He was *awake*. He'd probably been awake for ages. Please, don't let her have talked in her sleep. Or dribbled on him. Or done anything else embarrassing.

She mumbled something she hoped he'd take as an answer.

'Hangover?' he asked, sounding sympathetic.

How did he know? And actually, now she thought about it, what had he been doing, taking advantage of her when she'd been tipsy?

'Firstly, you were really knocking back the champagne last night.'

She cringed as she realised she'd spoken aloud. 'I had two glasses.'

'Correction. Your glass was topped up every time you took a sip, so you drank a *lot* more than you thought you were drinking. The waiters were what you might call unobtrusive.'

'Oh.' Well, that explained the hangover. Her fault, not his. But she genuinely hadn't realised how much she'd drunk.

'And, secondly, I didn't take advantage of you. I poured you into bed, yes—because you told me you were sleepy, and no way was I driving us back to London last night. If you'd felt sick in the middle of the M25, I couldn't have driven you to a safe place to throw up—not in time, anyway. And car valets don't work on Sundays.'

If her eyes hadn't already been closed, she would definitely have closed them in mortification. He was right. She probably *would* have been sick in his car. His precious car—which he loved more than any human being. She'd just bet he spent his off-duty hours polishing the chrome and nourishing the leather of the seats.

'I also didn't want you to wake in the night, feeling ill, in a strange place. So I stayed with you. I was planning to sleep in the chair, but when I tucked you in you asked me to give you a cuddle.'

Alyssa could have wept. Had she really been that pathetic?

'And two adults are perfectly capable of sharing a bed without having sex.'

So why hadn't they?

He must have guessed what she was thinking, because he said quietly, 'When a woman wraps her hand around a certain part of a man's anatomy and asks him to make love with her…he doesn't usually say no. Particularly if he likes sex as much as I do.'

Oh, no. It sounded as if he had photographic recall. This was bad—she was going to be embarrassed for the next thousand years! She wriggled away from him, desperate to put some space between them. At least he didn't try to keep her cuddled into him—though, on the other hand, that wasn't a good sign either. It meant he wanted space between them, too.

And they were miles and miles and miles away from London. And as he was her only way out of here… She had no choice. She had to rely on him to get her home.

'Just for the record, I insist that my partners are conscious and willing,' he said, still sounding amused, 'but I don't mind not being the one to make the first move.'

She'd asked him to make love with her. Actually, if she'd asked him for a cuddle, she'd probably *begged* him to make love to her. She remembered kissing him in the middle of the dance floor last night. Please, please, don't let a photographer have captured that or put it in the gossip rags. She'd never, ever live it down in the staffroom. Alyssa Ward, who didn't date, snogging the man who'd had more girlfriends than she'd had hot dinners.

And then a much, much nastier scenario filtered into her brain. Last night she'd been tipsy when she'd made love with Seb. So she hadn't thought about being sensible.

Panic struck her and she opened her eyes again. 'Please, tell me we used a…' She couldn't get the word out.

'A condom?' He didn't seem in the slightest bit embarrassed.

Well, he wouldn't. Heaven knew how many packets he'd bought over the years. He probably kept a stock of them in his wallet.

'Yes, we used a condom.'

Thank God.

'All four times,' he added.

Four times? Oh, no. This was really bad. 'We did it…four times?' She didn't remember that. Had she really acted like a sex-crazed, sex-starved…? Oh, words failed her!

He grinned. 'It would have been more, except I ran out of condoms.'

Her face was burning. He had to be teasing… Please, please, let him be teasing her.

Was it possible to have sex that many times in a night?

How many times *did* Seb usually have sex in a night?

She closed her eyes again, wishing the earth would open up and swallow her right now. 'Oh, God, I'm so sorry.'

'Alyssa.' His voice was soft. Full of laughter. 'I'm the one who should be saying sorry.'

For making love with her?

'For teasing you.' He stroked her cheek. 'Actually, we only did it twice.'

Which was bad enough. Once she could claim was a mistake. Twice—now, that was definitely on purpose.

The worst thing was, a little voice in the back of her head told her she wanted to do it again. Right now.

And that was a definite no-no. Even if she hadn't had a mammoth hangover.

'As you're awake, the bathroom's through the open door over there. Help yourself to whatever you need. There's a robe behind the door and a clean towel on the rail. Oh, and there's a new toothbrush in the cabinet.'

Alyssa felt the mattress move as he sat up. She turned her back, not daring to look at him. She knew for a fact he wasn't wearing anything. And Seb Radley, stark naked, was a lot more than she could cope with right now. 'Where are you going?' she asked. He wasn't going to desert her, was he?

'To get you some paracetamol and the Sebastian Radley hangover cure.'

Her panic subsided. Of course he wasn't going to strand her here. And she really, really wanted that paracetamol. 'Thank you.'

She waited until she heard the door close. Then she bolted out of bed and into the bathroom, where the mirror confirmed her worst suspicions. Panda eyes and bedhead hair. To say she looked a mess was an understatement. A huge understatement.

She groaned and stepped into the shower. Her head was still pounding, but having a shower and washing her hair made her feel better. The zingy citrus scent of Seb's shower gel helped to clear her thoughts. Cleaning her teeth made her feel better still. She wrapped Seb's bathrobe around herself—thick, fluffy, luxurious towelling—and walked back into the bedroom, intending to find her clothes and make herself decent before Seb came back.

But he was already there, lounging on the bed with a breakfast tray. He was wearing dark trousers and an open-necked white shirt—and he looked utterly edible. She could understand now why women lost their heads over him. She wasn't far off doing that herself right now.

And they'd had sex last night.

Twice.

Was it any wonder her knees felt like jelly?

'Paracetamol.' He handed her a glass of water and two white tablets, then patted the bed. 'Sit down.'

Being this close to Seb Radley—on a bed, with neither of them properly dressed—made her feel nervous. But she wasn't going to admit that to him.

She took the tablets—noting that the water was perfectly chilled—and replaced the empty glass on the tray.

'Have some juice.'

Freshly squeezed. 'Did you do this yourself?'

'I'm perfectly capable of working a juicer,' he said. 'How do you like your tea?'

'Strong enough to stand a spoon up in, with just a dash of milk, please.'

'Good. Same as me. I *detest* weak tea. Charlie makes the most vile tea in the universe. It's like dishwater.' He pulled a face. 'OK. Here you are. Toast, butter, marmalade, plain yoghurt and fresh pineapple.'

There was enough on the tray to feed an army. Surely he wasn't expecting her to eat all that?

And then she noticed that there were two plates. He was buttering granary toast liberally and adding marmalade. So he was having breakfast with her? Here? In his bedroom?

This was intimate in the extreme.

Though so was what they'd done last night.

She remembered exactly where his mouth had touched her. And how.

Alyssa tried to concentrate on the fresh pineapple and yoghurt he'd placed in a bowl for her. But she couldn't help noticing the buttery crumbs on his fingers. And she also couldn't help feeling the urge to lick them off his skin.

This was bad. Really bad. She wasn't supposed to feel like this about Seb. And she despised what he stood for—the constant bed-hopping, the lack of emotional commitment. According to him, it was 'fun'. He'd even suggesting proving it to her.

He'd certainly proved it last night.

She looked away before she did something stupid. Like stripping off the bathrobe she was wearing—*his* bathrobe— and begging him to make love with her again. Forget breakfast: what she wanted was Seb's body pushing into hers. Taking her back to the stars.

She shook herself mentally and finished her fruit. Weird— she'd thought she wouldn't be able to face food. But every mouthful made her feel better, and in the end she ate two pieces of buttered toast as well and accepted a second cup of tea.

'How do you feel?' he asked when she'd finished her breakfast.

'Better. A lot better,' she admitted.

'Guaranteed cure. Yoghurt and pineapple settle your stomach, the water and juice rehydrate you, and the tea and toast…' He grinned. 'That's just a bonus.'

The idea of Seb Radley having any kind of weakness—let alone for something as ordinary as tea and toast—surprised her. 'Well. Thank you for looking after me. And I'm sorry,' she said.

'What about?'

'Last night. Embarrassing you.'

He reached over and stroked her cheek. 'You didn't embarrass me, Alyssa. Or yourself. Don't worry about it.'

'I don't drink very often.'

'I should have guessed that. And I didn't look after you enough—at the very least, I should have warned you about the waiters.'

'And I've put everyone out, staying here.'

He shook his head. 'No, you haven't. This is my room.'

'*Your* room?' she asked, surprised.

'It's the family home. I don't live here any more—to be honest, I only usually come here when Mara's away—but this is still my room. Vicky has one, too.' His mouth thinned. 'By rights, Charlie's room should be the master suite. Except Mama Dearest and Barry-the-Wannabe-Baron are ensconced there.' He shook himself. 'But let's not talk about my family. They're not at all interesting.'

On the contrary. Alyssa thought that Seb's relationship with his family lay behind his relentless progression from one woman to the next. Then there was Seb's dislike of children. Now she thought about it, he tended to avoid paediatric cases on the ward.

Why?

She was about to ask, but his expression warned that he wasn't going to answer any more questions. 'I'm sorry about…well, putting you out.'

'You haven't put me out.' He frowned. 'Or if you mean about making you breakfast, I was hungry, too. I'm not in the mood for the breakfast room this morning. It suits me having a tray here.'

Because he didn't want anyone to know she'd stayed the night?

The question must have been written all over her face because his mouth thinned again. 'Because I've reached my politeness threshold. And I'm not giving my mother the satisfaction of a scene. I admit, I hadn't planned on staying here last night, but that's not because of you.'

Oh, no. Please, don't let him be thinking the wrong thing there. Don't let him be thinking that she was looking for a partner. Specifically, him.

'About last night...I don't usually, um, pounce on men.'

He gave her a lazy grin. 'You pounced very well.'

'We shouldn't have done it.'

'We're both single. No commitment. What's the problem?'

'We're not in a relationship.' And before he could get the wrong idea and back off at the speed of light, she added hurriedly, 'And we're not going to be.'

'Ah. That.' He shrugged. 'I promise to forget it, if you will. Now, I'm going to have a shower.'

I promise to forget it, if you will.

It sounded bad, Seb thought as he stepped beneath the shower and turned the water on. But what else could he have said? He'd seen the immediate disdain in her eyes. She despised him for sleeping around. And she thought she was just another notch on his bedpost.

Technically, he supposed, she was.

Except last night hadn't been a date. And Alyssa wasn't like any other woman he knew.

He could have taken her down to breakfast this morning. Had she been anyone else, he'd have brazened it out and not given a damn. But he'd wanted to spare Alyssa the knowing leers of Barry and the acid comments of Mara. Charlie and Sophie had spent their wedding night at a nearby hotel—very wisely, in Seb's view—and Vicky had left for London the previous night. Sure, there were other guests who'd stayed overnight whose table they could have joined, but everyone would expect the Radley son to sit with the family.

Family by name, but definitely not family by nature. He'd go to the ends of the earth for Charlie and Vicky—but Mara and Barry? No way. He wouldn't go to the end of the steps leading down from the house for them. They didn't deserve it.

So it had been easier to keep Alyssa here, in his room. Though that raised another problem. In more than one sense, he thought wryly, and turned the temperature of the water right down.

What he really wanted to do now was walk out of the shower—to hell with the water—and strip that robe from her, tumble her onto his bed and make love with her until neither of them could see straight. But he also knew that would be a bad move. She was running scared.

And all he wanted to do was to stop her feeling frightened. Make her forget everything except him.

This was bad. He didn't *do* protective male.

If she'd been one of his usual women, she wouldn't be in the bedroom now. She'd be in the shower with him, her back against the tiles and his body thrusting into hers. A farewell performance.

But she wasn't his woman. Wasn't like any other woman he'd known. And he really wasn't sure how to deal with this. Though at least the cold water worked, so when he climbed out of the shower he could get dressed and return to Alyssa looking completely normal, not as if he had a raging case of lust. She was already dressed when he came out of the bathroom, but she looked distinctly uncomfortable. He could guess why. 'Sorry, I should have mentioned it before I had a shower. I raided my sister's room on the way back from the kitchen.'

'Vicky's still here?'

He shook his head. 'But she won't mind. I borrowed some underwear for you as you're about the same size.'

'Thank you.'

Lord, she looked pretty when she blushed. He was almost tempted to tease her, keep her all pink and pretty for a bit longer. Except that wasn't fair. He wanted her to feel at ease here—not awkward. Besides, if he started to think about how pretty she looked, he'd start to wonder how pink and pretty she'd look with her clothes off. 'Lighten up. You don't look that creased.'

'Thanks to you, because you hung my dress up.'

She sounded surprised, as if she hadn't expected him to be that thoughtful.

'If you'd slept in your dress, it would have been completely crumpled, and I didn't want you to be embarrassed this morning.' Seb raked a hand through his hair. 'Look, last night—it was a one-off. Too much champagne, too much—' He stopped. Too much emotion. What was he thinking? Lack of, more like. He didn't *do* emotion. 'We're adults.'

'I'm not trying to trap you, Seb. I don't want a relationship with you.'

That stung. But he knew he deserved it. And he couldn't offer her a relationship anyway. It wasn't how he operated. 'How about friendship?'

'Friendship?'

'Yes.' He smiled wryly. 'I never thought I'd suggest that to a woman who was single. But I'd like us to be friends. No strings. Just friends.'

'And we'll forget about last night.'

He was going to have a hard time forgetting how it had felt to make love with her, how soft her skin was, how she tasted, but… 'Yes.'

'OK.' She looked relieved. What had she expected? That he'd completely ignore her?

'I'll take the tray down to Cook while you, um, finish getting changed,' he said.

'Cook? You have a *cook*?'

'Strictly speaking, she's Mara's cook. But she's been with us for years. She used to spoil me when I was a kid.' He smiled. 'For your information, I wasn't intending to just dump the tray on her. I'm capable of loading a dishwasher.'

'Right.' She didn't look convinced.

'I know my way around a kitchen. Actually, I make a fabulous chicken Dijon.' His best weapon of seduction: set a candle-lit table, cook a meal—and let your female companion see you preparing it, too, so she knew you hadn't just got it delivered from a restaurant ready to heat up, or had bought it from the supermarket—and she'd be putty in your hands.

She gave him a look as if she knew exactly what he was thinking. Fine. He wasn't going to let on about the rest of it. The fact that, after Julia, he'd stayed with Charlie for a week and cooked his brother a meal every night, to make sure that Charlie actually ate something. *That* was personal.

'I'll be back in ten minutes,' he said. 'Then we can go.'

'Sure. I'll be ready.'

He believed her. She wasn't the sort who'd make a fuss. Quiet, efficient and practical, that was Alyssa.

And he'd try very hard not to think of the rest of it. Sensual, responsive and—

No.

CHAPTER NINE

'SHOULDN'T we say goodbye to—?' Alyssa began.

'Mara and Barry?' Seb shrugged. 'No need. I've already seen them.'

And it hadn't been a pleasant encounter, Alyssa guessed. It felt rude to go without at least saying goodbye—particularly as she'd been an unexpected overnight guest—but the set of Seb's mouth warned her not to push the issue. And in some respects it didn't matter if Mara and Barry thought her uncouth, because she wouldn't be meeting them again. She and Seb were colleagues, not an item, and his mother and stepfather were hardly likely to turn up at the Docklands Memorial Hospital.

Seb drove them back towards London in near silence. Driving on the motorway seemed to calm him a little, and eventually he sighed. 'I'm sorry, Alyssa. I didn't mean to be offhand with you this morning. Mara just brings out the worst in me, and right now I don't like myself very much.'

Because of last night? Well, she'd been as much to blame for that. More, in fact. She'd been the one to pounce. 'You're not as bad as you like to think you are,' she said quietly.

He grinned. 'Careful, Alyssa. You might be close to polishing my ego. And that would never do.' He gave her a sidelong look. 'Do you have to rush back to London?'

'No.' She was only going back to the housework—which wasn't her favourite occupation anyway.

'Want to have lunch with me? Not as a date,' he added, a shade too quickly for her liking.

She'd already told him she wasn't looking for a relationship. What did she have to do to prove it? 'Lunch is fine, as long as you let me pay for it.' Seb had refused to let her give him any money towards the cost of petrol, saying that he'd have had to go with or without her. And that had grated: she didn't want him to think of her as just another woman out for what she could get.

Because not all women were like that.

He just had to work it out for himself.

'Let you pay for it?' he echoed, sounding surprised.

'That's what *friends* do,' she emphasised. 'Take turns.'

'In that case, thank you. I accept.' His dimple reappeared briefly. 'Do I get to choose the venue?'

'Whatever.' She hoped she sounded more casual than she felt.

'Good. I know this little pub by the river…' He smiled wryly. 'Ah, listen to me. Pathetic. But after being near Mara, I need something soothing. I want comfort food and comfort surroundings.'

'And you like being near the river?'

He nodded. 'When I lose a patient, I normally end up walking by the Thames. Doesn't matter where. Just being near water calms me. And I prefer rivers to the sea.'

Because they were more controllable?

Not that she was going to ask him that.

He turned off the motorway at the next junction and drove through some narrow, winding roads. A few minutes later they were parked outside a pub with whitewashed walls, mullioned windows and a thatched roof.

'Is this your normal stopping place on the way back to London?' Alyssa asked.

'Something like that. The beer's good—not that I'm going to have a beer right now, as I'm driving—and the food's excellent.'

'Comfort food', in Seb's view, turned out to be pasta filled with pecorino and asparagus with extra Parmesan grated on the top, a hunk of ciabatta bread with olive oil and balsamic vinegar for dipping, and a creamy dessert.

When the waitress had taken their order, she said, 'Seb, your arteries—'

'Don't get hammered like this very often,' he cut in with a grin.

Hmm. They'd had three meals together now—four, if you counted breakfast in his bed—and this was the third where he'd chosen a cream-laden pudding. And he'd been very liberal with the butter on his toast that morning.

Ha. And now she was sounding like a worried wife. Which was totally inappropriate: Seb would never get married, and even if he did she wouldn't be in the running as a potential bride. She didn't intend to mess up her life again with a wedding ring either.

'Oh, this is better. Much, much better,' he said when they were sitting under the willow trees next to the water, and there was an enormous plate of pasta in front of him. 'Mmm. I might even be human again by the time we get back to London.'

'You really dislike your mother that much?' Alyssa couldn't imagine how that would feel. She'd never felt anything other than deep love and respect for her own mother.

Seb tore off a hunk of bread. 'Let's change the subject.'

Alyssa tried not to watch him dipping the bread into the oil. Precise and definite, just as his hands were when he worked with patients. And just as his hands had been on her body last night, seeming to know exactly how and where she liked being touched.

But they weren't going back there. Even though it had definitely rated as one of the most pleasurable experiences of her life.

'So, as we're friends, are you going to tell me?' he asked.

Alyssa gave a guilty start. 'Tell you what?' What she'd been thinking? Wild horses wouldn't drag *that* from her.

'Why you hate weddings.'

Oh. That. 'No.'

'Love of your life married someone else?' he guessed.

Caught off guard, she admitted, 'He married me. Except—' Oh, no, what *was* she saying? She'd sworn she would never tell anyone in London about that.

'Alyssa, we're friends,' Seb said softly. 'I'm going to respect your confidences as much as you've already respected mine.'

And he probably *had* told her more than he'd told anyone else. He'd let her close to his family. Although he'd been at pains to make sure she realised it wasn't because he was madly in love with her, he'd let her close to him.

His eyes were absolutely sincere. And, yes, she could trust him with this.

'Just don't laugh at me,' she muttered.

'Laugh at you?' He sounded shocked. 'Of course I won't.'

She hoped not. 'I was twenty-five. Very, very naïve. I met Scott at a party and he swept me off my feet.' She sighed. 'I thought I was in love with Scott, and I thought he was in love with me. My mum wasn't so sure, but I didn't listen to her. I was convinced he was The One.' And how wrong she'd been. 'When he asked me to marry him, I said yes. Mum said we ought to wait for a bit, get engaged and take it slowly, but I…' She'd wanted a family. A big family. Like the one she'd never

had when she'd been growing up—no dad, plus old-fash-
ioned grandparents who'd disowned her mother as soon as
they'd found out Kathy was pregnant, and the rest of the family had followed suit. Alyssa had never known her aunts, un-
cles and cousins either. 'Scott said there wasn't any reason to
wait. So we booked the register office for as soon as we
could.'

'So your mum didn't come to the wedding?'

She stared at him in surprise. 'Of course she did! She
didn't approve, but she wouldn't have missed my wedding.
Not for anything.' And Kathy had been there afterwards to
pick up the pieces when it had all gone so badly wrong.

'Scott was a doctor?' Seb guessed.

'Pharmaceutical rep. He was taking a part-time course—
his bosses let him have one day a week as study leave, and he'd
managed to find a course that was on Fridays and weekends.
Because it was part time, it was all year round instead of just
during normal academic terms.' She shrugged. 'It meant we
couldn't see as much of each other as we wanted, but it was
only going to be for a couple of years. And it meant he'd have
much better chances of promotion.' And then they'd move to
a bigger house and start a family: that had been the plan.

Thank God it hadn't gone that far.

'Lucky timing,' Seb said dryly. 'Course in London, was it?'

'Birmingham.'

'Which is where you worked at the time?'

She shook her head. 'Newcastle. So it was a bit too far to
commute. He went to Birmingham on Thursday nights for the
whole weekend. But it was OK. I used to work late shifts on
Friday and Saturday, and he'd be back late on Sunday nights.'

'And he cheated on you while he was away?' Seb asked
quietly.

Alyssa took a deep breath. Even now, years later, the sick feeling of shame still enveloped her when she thought about it. How stupid she'd been. How gullible and trusting and *stupid*. 'No. It turned out *I* was the other woman,' she said, her voice barely more than a croak. 'He was already married to someone else when he married me.' So her marriage had been a sham. She hadn't even *been* married, in the eyes of the law. And Scott hadn't tried to get a divorce before marrying her—it hadn't been a question of a mistake in some paperwork. He'd been married Alyssa had been a bigamist's dupe.

Seb looked sympathetic. 'That's rough. How did you find out?'

'She—' Even now, Alyssa couldn't bring herself to say *Scott's wife* '—found my number on his mobile phone. She rang me and asked me what the hell I thought I was doing, having an affair with her husband. And I said I didn't know what she was talking about—I was married to Scott, and who on earth was she? That's when it came out. He'd told her he was on a course in Newcastle on Monday to Thursday—when he was with me. And he was with her on Thursday to Sunday, when he told me he was on a course in Birmingham. He'd duped us both.'

'Lowlife bastard,' Seb growled.

Part of Alyssa was surprised. She'd been half expecting Seb to—well, if not admire exactly, at least appreciate the way Scott had managed to weave his two 'lives' together so credibly.

'I hope your dad took him apart.'

Ah. Now there was the rub. She stared at the table. 'I don't have a dad. Never have. It's just me and my mum.'

Instantly, he looked contrite. 'I'm sorry. I just assumed… well, that other people were luckier than me.'

Alyssa heard the momentary hint of wistfulness in his voice and looked up. 'How old were you when your dad died?'

'Fourteen.' He shrugged. 'Not a huge deal. We weren't that close.'

But Seb had wanted to be. As the spare and not the heir, he probably wouldn't have had as much of his father's attention as Charlie had done. And if his mother had been desperate for a daughter, the chances were that she wouldn't have paid Seb much attention, either once Vicky had been born.

Was that why Seb didn't believe in relationships—or like kids?

And fourteen was a very tough age to lose a parent. Which made her wonder... 'Was it an accident?' she asked.

'Heart attack.'

And that explained everything. Every time Seb saved a patient in Resus, it was making up for the fact that nobody had saved his dad. He hadn't chosen that particularly career path so he could remain detached. He'd chosen it to save others from going through what he'd gone through. And he disliked children because it reminded him of how unhappy he'd been as a child.

It was all so obvious. But why hadn't anyone put the pieces together before? Why hadn't anyone made Seb feel that he came first in their life?

Or maybe that was why he never let anyone close. If you didn't let them near enough, they couldn't reject you. And if you were always the one who called a halt after the first date, then you would never be dumped.

'I'm sorry,' she said quietly.

'Not your fault. Not anybody's. And this is getting just a little too deep for me,' Seb said.

She'd thought him shallow. Now she knew it was a very carefully polished surface. And Seb wouldn't allow anyone close enough to look below that surface.

Although he'd let *her* that close.

'Let's talk about something less…' She couldn't think of the right word. Painful? Disturbing?

But he seemed to know what she meant. He switched back to being Seb the Socialite, charming and witty. And although he was good company, part of her missed the hidden Seb. The one who'd admitted to his real feelings. The one who'd lost himself in her body last night.

A shiver of pleasure snaked down her spine at the memory—a shiver she didn't manage to suppress quickly enough.

'Cold?' Seb asked.

'A little,' Alyssa lied.

'Let's forget pudding.' He gave her a smile—one that didn't reach his eyes, she noticed. 'Let's go.'

He didn't say much on the drive back to London. And Alyssa, wishing she hadn't given in to the impulse to tell him about Scott—wishing she hadn't shown Seb just how gullible she'd been—was happy not to say much either. Finally, he pulled up outside her flat.

Was this where she was supposed to ask him in for coffee? Had he been anyone else—had they not had that conversation at the pub—she would have asked him in. But this was Seb. She didn't want him to think she was chasing him. Because she wasn't. 'I, um…thanks for the lift,' she said, hating this new awkwardness between them. 'I'll return Vicky's things to you when I've washed them.'

'Whenever.'

She climbed out of the car. 'See you at work, then.'

'Sure. And, Alyssa?' he added, just as she was about to close the door.

Her heart gave a weird little leap. 'Yes?'

'What we talked about today…I won't be telling anyone else about it.'

What had she expected? That he'd ask her to stay with him a bit longer? That he'd ask her if he could come in for coffee? Ridiculous. She shoved the feeling of disappointment to one side. He wasn't going to betray her trust, and that was the main thing. 'Me neither,' she said.

As before, he waited until she was safely indoors before he drove off. Good manners. He probably couldn't wait to get away.

'Don't try fooling yourself. He's not for you,' she told herself crisply.

Though showering and changing didn't make her feel any better. She couldn't quite shake off this weird, gloomy feeling. It took her the rest of the day to work out what the feeling was—and, when she did, she was horrified. It couldn't be. Shouldn't be.

And yet she had to face it. She'd fallen for Seb. And the flatness she felt was just because *he* wasn't around.

'Absolutely not,' Alyssa told herself, scowling at the shirt she was ironing. She'd promised herself she'd never let anyone have the chance to humiliate her again, the way Scott had. And falling in love with Seb Radley was a passport to humiliation. He didn't want a serious relationship—and if he had any idea how she felt about him he'd run a mile. And there would be pitying looks at her all the way through the hospital—just as there'd been for the string of women who'd fallen for Seb and discovered he really meant it about 'no relationships'. Heartache City, here she came.

Which meant she needed to get some distance back between them.

Starting now.

* * *

Why, why, why had he told Alyssa so much? Seb scowled and dug another spoonful from the tub of rich maple walnut ice cream. He knew she was perceptive. He knew she'd be able to guess most of what he hadn't told her—what he hadn't told anyone, even Charlie and Vicky. Stupid, to bare his soul like that to someone. The surest way to get hurt.

But she'd told him things, too. About her dad and her disastrous marriage. And he could understand now why she didn't date. When someone knocked your trust that much… No wonder she didn't approve of his social life either.

The thing that worried him most, though, was the way he'd felt all protective about her. He just didn't *do* that sort of thing. Saturday night had been a mistake. They were agreed on that. Neither of them was interested in a relationship.

So why couldn't he get her out of his head?

Alyssa managed to avoid Seb for the next day or two. Their duties didn't coincide, and when they were in the department at the same time they were both busy.

On the Wednesday, just before lunch, she saw Seb heading towards her, but before he could say anything Anton, their new house officer, came out of cubicles.

'Alyssa—help?'

'Sure.' She smiled at him, and was relieved to notice that Seb had seen her being buttonholed and had gone away again. Good. She wasn't ready to face him yet. 'What's the problem, Anton?'

'Patient came in after being knocked off her bike. But I can't get her nosebleed to stop, or the cut on her shin, and I don't like the look of her elbow—it looks puffy to me. Bruised.' Anton shook his head. 'Haemophiliacs are male, so I can rule that out.'

'It might be another blood-clotting disorder,' Alyssa said.
'So what do I do?'

'Blood tests, among other things,' Alyssa said. 'Let's go and have a chat with your patient.' She followed Anton back into the cubicle. 'Hi, I'm Alyssa Ward, the registrar in ED. Anton's a bit concerned about you. Would you mind if I ask you a few questions?'

'Sure.' The patient was still trying to stem her nosebleed.

'Lean forward,' Alyssa directed gently, 'because that will stop the blood running down your throat.'

'Pressure on the bridge?' Anton said.

Alyssa nodded. 'And a cold compress on that shin—well done for elevating it.' She glanced quickly at the notes. 'Ruth—may I call you Ruth?' At the girl's nod, she continued, 'Does anyone in your family have blood-clotting problems?'

'I'm adopted. I wouldn't know,' Ruth said.

And it would explain why Ruth maybe hadn't been tested for blood disorders before. 'Do you get nosebleeds often?'

'Quite a lot. It's a nuisance,' Ruth said, 'especially when it happens at work. Still, at least everyone knows who to come to when they need a tissue.'

'How about your gums?' Alyssa asked. 'Any bleeding there?'

'The dentist said I need to use a softer brush—I had a few problems with bleeding, but he thought it was because I'd brushed my teeth too hard.'

'And your periods?'

'They're a bit heavy,' Ruth admitted.

'I'd like to run some blood tests,' Alyssa said, 'because I think you may have a blood-clotting disorder called von Willebrand's disease.'

Ruth's eyes widened. 'Is it serious?'

'We can do something about it—the hard part is diagnosing it,' Alyssa said. 'Can I ask, are you planning to have children?'

'I've just got engaged. Josh and I were thinking about it maybe in a year or so...' Ruth's voice faded as the implications sank in. 'Are you telling me I can't have kids?'

'No, just that if you do have von Willebrand's disease, it's what we call an autosomal dominant trait—it affects girls as well as boys, so if you have it your children will have a fifty per cent change of inheriting it.'

'So what is von Willebrand's disease?'

Alyssa glanced at Anton, who pulled a 'please don't ask me to explain it' face. She gave him a slight nod to acknowledge it, then turned to Ruth. 'It's where your body doesn't have enough of a protein called von Willebrand's factor,' Alyssa explained. 'If you damage a blood vessel—say you come off your bike and knock your shin—the blood cells that make clots in your blood work with something called clotting factor, and they plug the hole and stop the bleeding. With von Willebrand's disease, the process doesn't work properly so the platelets don't stick together, and the bleeding doesn't stop as quickly as it should.'

'Is it going to kill me?' Ruth asked, looking worried. 'Am I going to die young?'

'Not from von Willebrand's disease,' Alyssa said. 'We can give you something to treat it so your blood will clot properly. What we give you depends on what the blood tests say, but if it's not too severe we can give you a nasal spray called DDAVP or desmopressin acetate. That boosts your level of factor eight—the clotting mechanism. If it is von Willebrand's disease, I'll refer you to a haematologist, who can talk through all the options with you.'

Ruth's nose finally stopped bleeding, and she took the tissue away. 'I'm going to have to break my engagement,' she said dully.

'Why?'

'I can't make our kids inherit something like this—I can't do that to Josh.' Her eyes brimmed with tears.

'Hey.' Alyssa sat down beside her. 'Give your man a chance to have a say, too. It may be that he'd rather have you with no kids than have kids with someone else who isn't you.' She squeezed Ruth's hands. 'And, yes, you'll need closer monitoring during pregnancy, but it really doesn't mean you can't have kids. Don't do anything drastic. Have a chat with the haematologist and a genetic counsellor before you make any decisions. Medicine changes all the time—we can treat conditions now that we thought were incurable ten years ago.'

Ruth nodded. 'I wish my mum was here.'

'No problem,' Alyssa said softly. 'I'll call her for you. And I want to take a closer look at your elbow—that looks painful.'

'It is,' Ruth admitted.

'I'll call your mum while Anton takes some blood samples,' Alyssa said. 'Anton, we need platelet count, template bleeding time, von Willebrand factor level and factor VIII activity.'

Anton nodded. 'I'll do it now.'

'Try not to worry, Ruth,' Alyssa said softly.

'I only came in because I was knocked off my bike,' Ruth said. 'Now…' She shook her head. 'I can't take all this in.'

'You'll be fine. And it'll help to have your mum here—someone you can rely on,' Alyssa said. 'Do you want me to call your fiancé as well?'

'Not until I've talked to Mum,' Ruth said. 'But thank you.'

'That's what I'm here for.'

* * *

It'll help to have your mum here—someone you can rely on.

No and no, in his case, Seb thought as he passed the cubicle where Alyssa was treating her patient. Mara would be hopeless—and she also wasn't someone you could rely on. Alyssa's views on family were so different from his own. She got on well with her mum, whereas he didn't like most of his family—with the exception of Charlie, Vicky and his new sister-in-law. And Alyssa had sounded slightly wistful when she'd talked to Ruth about children. Yet another reason why it couldn't work between them: he didn't want children.

Maybe he should take a step back on the overtures of friendship. The last thing he wanted was to give her the wrong impression—to let her think that he wanted to be more than friends.

Time, he thought, to get his little black book out. Go on a few dates. Put some distance between him and Alyssa.

That way, he'd be safe.

CHAPTER TEN

YET *another* blonde nurse. There couldn't be any more left in the hospital, so Seb must be working his way through the bank staff now, Alyssa thought grumpily as she joined the canteen queue and saw Seb laughing and flirting at a table across the room.

For the last month he'd really kept his distance from her. He was perfectly polite to her at work—and he'd been pleasant enough when she'd returned his sister's things, laundered—but on departmental nights out he always made sure he sat as far away from her as possible. He hadn't asked her to have lunch with him, even if they'd been taking a break at the same time, and she was fairly sure he'd been avoiding her in the staffroom as well.

Obviously he'd had second thoughts about being friends with her and regretted the way he'd confided in her. Well, if that was the way he wanted it, fine. She could be adult about what had happened between them, even if he couldn't.

But somehow she couldn't face the canteen right now. It wasn't just Seb. The room felt sticky, oppressive, and the cooking smells made her feel queasy. Plus, there wasn't anything on the menu she fancied. What she *really* wanted was freshly squeezed orange juice, strawberries and a Marmite sandwich.

So today she'd skip the canteen—a walk to the parade of shops near the hospital and a bit of fresh air would do her good.

The bakery and the greengrocer's were fine, though she found herself almost gagging in the queue at the deli. The woman in front of her was wearing way too much perfume and the strong scent was overpowering. That, and the smell of coffee beans being ground.

Oh, for goodness' sake. Anyone would think she was pregnant, being sensitive to smells like that. And of course she wasn't. She'd been celibate since Scott.

Except for that night with Seb. A month ago.

Suddenly, alarm bells clanged in her head. *A month ago.* Which meant her last period had been... She calculated the date rapidly.

Six weeks ago.

Even stress didn't disrupt her menstrual cycle: she came on every twenty-eight days precisely. She could tell when her period would start, virtually to the hour. Now she was two weeks late.

And she was sensitive to smells.

And she was being picky about food.

And she'd been feeling very, very tired recently—which she'd put down to working long hours.

And her breasts felt sore.

Whoa, there. They weren't tell-tale signs. She *couldn't* be pregnant. Seb had used a condom. This was all psychosomatic—like being a medical student, when you read up on a disease you'd covered in lectures and then convinced yourself that you had all the symptoms. She was just thinking about the signs of early pregnancy and imagining that they applied to her. She couldn't be pregnant. They'd used protection.

Well, Seb had *said* he'd used a condom, and she was sure he wouldn't have lied about something as important as that. Then again, she also knew that the only one hundred per cent effective form of contraception was abstinence. Supposing one of the condoms had been faulty?

No. Of course she wasn't pregnant. She was panicking over nothing. They'd made love twice, using a condom. Even if one *had* been faulty, the chances of her getting pregnant weren't that high. One in four, on average, if she made love during the most fertile part of her cycle.

Though four weeks *ago* had been the most fertile part of her cycle.

She took a deep breath. Right now there was something she needed far more than she needed lunch.

A testing kit.

She knew it would be negative—she just wanted to put her mind at rest, that was all.

She bought the kit hurriedly, hoping that nobody she knew would come into the shop and see what she was buying. Stuffed it into the bottom of her handbag, where nobody was likely to see it. And she'd intended to use it as soon as she got back to the department—except Resus was full because there had been a car accident nearby when she'd been on her lunch-break, and the paramedics had brought in two ambulances full. Whiplash, a banged head with momentary loss of consciousness that definitely needed investigation with a scan and what turned out to be a tension pneumothorax.

In the end Alyssa didn't get the chance to use the kit until she got home. The nearer she got to her front door, the heavier her handbag felt, dragging her down.

She couldn't be pregnant.

She *couldn't* be expecting Seb's child.

Could she?

She locked the front door behind her, slid the security chain across, dug the kit from her bag and did the test.

According to the instructions, she'd know the results within two minutes.

They were the longest two minutes of her life. She sat watching the two windows of the test, checking the clock every so often to see how many seconds had passed.

Tick. Tick. Tick.

One blue line: that proved the test was working.

Tick. Tick. Tick.

Don't let it be two. Don't let it be two. Don't let it be two.

She glanced up at the clock. Thirty seconds to go.

And then she glanced back down. In that moment when she'd checked the clock, another line had appeared.

Positive.

She rushed back into her bathroom and was immediately sick.

After Alyssa had washed her face, cleaned her teeth and taken a couple of sips of chilled water, she sat down at her kitchen table.

She was pregnant.

With Seb's baby.

He didn't want children. She was concentrating on her career. There wasn't going to be a happy ending.

Which meant…what? She should have a termination?

She realised that she was already holding her hands protectively across her abdomen, and smiled ruefully. No, that wasn't an option. This baby wasn't planned, but it wasn't unwanted. And she had a great role model: her own mother had brought her up single-handedly.

So she was going to keep the baby.

OK. That was the most important decision made.

Now she had to tell Seb. She wasn't looking forward to it. No doubt he'd think she was just trying to trap him into marriage, even though she wasn't. But *not* telling him wasn't an option. Apart from the fact that he had a right to know, the pregnancy would start to show in three or four months and he was bright enough to work out the dates for himself. Better to tell him sooner rather than later.

So what was she going to say to him—to the man who'd made it very clear he didn't like children and didn't want any of his own?

I'm pregnant. It's yours. I'm keeping it. And I don't expect anything from you.

That was a bit too blunt, even for Seb.

She walked over to her dresser and took a pad of paper and a pen from a drawer.

Forty minutes later, the top of the table was covered in screwed-up drafts that didn't sound right. But the sheet of paper that counted was neatly folded in an envelope addressed to Seb. She wasn't chancing this one in the post: she'd deliver it in person. With any luck, he'd be out so she'd have time to get things completely straight in her head before she had to face him.

Quietly, she locked the flat behind her and headed for her car.

Crunch.

Junk mail. Probably stuff for the council elections, Seb thought as he switched the light on, ready to scoop up the papers from his doormat and put them straight in the recycling box.

Except junk mail didn't come in a plain envelope with his name handwritten on the front.

Frowning, he ripped the seal open, unfolded the letter and read it.

He had to read it through twice more before it hit him.

Alyssa was pregnant. With *their* baby.

And she'd told him by letter!

Scowling, he grabbed the phone. What the hell was she playing at, leaving him a letter like this? Why hadn't she just told him face to face?

He ignored the fact that he'd been avoiding her—and trying to forget her with a string of dates. Dates that hadn't worked, because he hadn't gone beyond the kissing stage with any of them. He hadn't wanted to go that far even. And that hadn't done much for his temper. He'd refused to let himself think about *why* he hadn't wanted to kiss another woman.

He flicked through his electronic diary for Alyssa's number, then noticed what the time was.

A quarter to two in the morning.

Now wasn't a reasonable time to ring her. Particularly as she was in the early stages of pregnancy and needed her sleep. But tomorrow morning, first thing, he'd haul her into his office. And he'd get a proper explanation from her.

I don't expect anything from you, indeed.

Except Alyssa was already busy on the ward when he got there. 'She's in cubicles with a patient,' Tracey said, giving Seb a curious look which he deliberately ignored.

'Any particular cubicle?' he asked.

'Three, I think.'

'Thanks.' He strode over to Cubicle Three and peered in round the curtain. Alyssa was there, talking to a woman; a teenage boy was lying on the bed, looking pale and exhausted.

'Excuse me. Dr Ward, a word?' he said coolly.

Alyssa went white when she saw him. 'Is it urgent?'

He glanced at the teenager and sighed inwardly. 'When you've finished, then. My office.'

She nodded, but there was a definite note of defiance in her eyes. She'd made her position clear in her letter.

Well, he'd had a sleepless night to think about his position. And he didn't agree with anything she'd said. When she finally showed up in his office, he was going to be more than ready to handle any arguments she came up with. This was one fight he wasn't intending to lose. They were going to do the right thing by this baby, and that was that.

He gave her a brooding stare, then forced himself to smile at her patient and the patient's mother. 'I'm sorry for interrupting,' he said quietly, and closed the curtain again.

Seb had looked far from pleased. Then again, what else had Alyssa expected? She'd just delivered his worst nightmare: the news that he was going to be a dad. Seb, who couldn't bear children and didn't want a family.

And, knowing his jaundiced views, he probably didn't believe that she'd meant it when she'd said she didn't want anything from him. He probably thought she was going to sue him for child maintenance payments, and as much money as she could screw out of him besides.

Well, she'd just have to put him straight. After she'd finished with her patient.

Taking a deep breath, she focused on her job. 'How long has Graham had the rash?' she asked.

'A few days. It wasn't like this at first, though—it looked more like a sweat rash. I did start to panic that it was meningitis, but he had the vaccination,' Mrs Webster said. 'And he wasn't complaining of a headache or a stiff neck.'

Obviously the meningitis cards handed out by the health promotion people were being read, Alyssa thought. Good.

'He hasn't got meningitis, has he?' Mrs Webster looked distraught.

Alyssa couldn't rule it out for certain. You didn't always get all the symptoms of a disease, and she didn't like the look of the rash. 'Let's have a look,' she said quietly.

She pressed the skin, but the rash didn't fade. Which meant Graham was bleeding under the skin. The rash, known as purpura, was either due to meningococcaemia or a virus—either Henoch-Schönlein or thrombocytopenia, though she'd need to do a blood test to check the blood platelets before she could make a firm diagnosis.

'He said his knees hurt, but I thought it was probably growing pains. I was going to make him an appointment with our family doctor, then he said this morning that his stomach really hurt, and I thought I'd better bring him here.'

'Good idea. May I examine you, Graham?' Alyssa asked.

The teenager nodded, still wincing in pain.

She examined him gently. No sign of guarding in the lower quadrants and there was also no sign of a palpable mass in his abdomen, so it wasn't intussusception, a condition where the small bowel had telescoped. 'I'm pretty sure it's not appendicitis. Graham, I know this is going to be hideously embarrassing, but there's one more test I need to do to make absolutely sure it's not your appendix—a rectal exam. I could get a male doctor to do that, if you'd rather?' she offered.

He shook his head. 'It's all right.'

From his face, she could see that he just wanted the pain to stop and life to go back to normal. Poor kid. 'OK, sweetheart. Would you mind rolling over onto your stomach?'

A rectal examination told her what she needed to know.

She removed her gloves. 'OK, I'm pleased to say we can rule that out. But I'd like you to give me a urine sample.' She handed him the container. 'I'll wait outside with your mum.' The least she could do was give him a little bit of dignity back. 'Give us a yell when you're ready.'

'What do you think it is?' Mrs Webster asked when they'd stepped outside the curtains. 'Please, tell me it's not meningitis.' Tears glistened in her eyes. 'I couldn't bear it if I lost him. He's all I've got.'

'Can I ask, did the rash start on his lower legs?' A symmetrical, bruise-like rash on both legs, together with stomach pain and joint pain, pointed very strongly to one condition. Particularly if it started on his lower legs.

Mrs Webster nodded. 'Is it serious?'

'I think Graham has something called Henoch-Schönlein purpura, which we normally call HSP for short,' Alyssa explained. 'It's an allergic condition that causes the small blood vessels to become inflamed. Sometimes it affects your skin—that's why Graham's got a rash—and sometimes it affects your joints, your kidneys and your stomach. I'd expect there to be traces of blood in that urine sample.'

'Is it catching?' Mrs Webster asked. 'Could he have picked it up from one of his friends?'

Alyssa shook her head. 'And we don't always know what causes it. Sometimes it's because of an infection, sometimes it's a reaction to medication, and sometimes it's caused by a food allergy. Is he allergic to anything that you know about, or is he taking any medication?'

'There's no allergies on either side of the family,' Mrs Webster said, 'and he hasn't been on any medication.'

'Then I think it's likely to be caused by bacterium—most likely a form of streptococcus, but there are one or two others that can cause it,' Alyssa said. 'I'll want to do some blood tests, too.' Creatinine and nitrogen levels were affected by HSP, though she also wanted to do an antibody nuclear test in case it was systemic lupus erythematosus, a condition that had several similar symptoms. 'I'm going to send him for an ultrasound, too, to check there aren't any problems in his stomach that the surgeon might need to see, and I'll need to take a sample of his skin to send to the lab—that'll confirm the diagnosis.'

'But he's going to be all right?'

There were complications, but they were rare—and fatal complications were even rarer. 'He should be. It's what we call a self-limiting condition—that means it will get better on its own in four to six weeks, but it can flare up again. I'd also recommend that you see your GP every few days for a urine test and a blood test so we can keep an eye on Graham and make sure his kidneys are functioning properly.'

'He's not going to…' Mrs Webster stopped, as if saying the word might be bad luck. 'I'm sorry. I know I'm fussing, but he's all I've got since his dad left me,' she added, pitching her voice low so her son couldn't hear.

This could be me in fifteen years' time, Alyssa thought. On my own in hospital with our child, worried sick and having to cope because Seb left me for a string of blondes.

Except it wouldn't be her. Seb wouldn't leave her—because she wasn't giving him the chance to be with her in the first place.

'He should be fine,' she reassured Mrs Webster. 'We can give him some pain relief—though studies have shown that giving corticosteroids doesn't have much effect, so I'm not going to prescribe anything else for him.'

'The thing is, he's got his exams next month.'

Alyssa knew instantly what she meant. 'And this isn't the best time to be missing school. I'm sure we can do something to help.'

'I've finished,' Graham called.

Alyssa labelled the sample, took some bloods and labelled those, then gave Graham some pain relief. 'The bloods should be back in about an hour. If you'd like to go and have a cup of coffee or something and then come back, I'll have everything sorted ready for your GP,' she said.

'Thanks,' Mrs Webster said, smiling and looking less panicky.

Alyssa wished *she* felt less panicky. But, right now, she had to face Seb.

And she really, really wasn't looking forward to this conversation.

CHAPTER ELEVEN

WHEN he heard the rap on the door, Seb stopped dictating letters and switched off the machine. 'Come in.'

As he'd hoped, it was Alyssa.

About time, too. He'd been so frustrated and impatient he'd been ready to tear the hospital down with his bare hands. 'Dr Ward. Close the door behind you,' Seb drawled. 'And lock it. I don't want any interruptions.' He switched his phone through to his secretary, then took it off the hook to be absolutely certain that nobody was going to interrupt them.

'But—'

'But nothing, Alyssa.'

When she'd done as he asked, he continued, 'I want an explanation. Now.'

She leaned against the door and folded her arms. 'You've already had one.'

'Your letter? I expected better from you—not the coward's way out.'

Her eyes narrowed. 'I'm not a coward.'

'So why didn't you tell me yourself?'

'Because when you're here, you're busy.'

Plus, he supposed, the middle of the hospital wasn't the

right place to talk about something that personal. Not with a hospital grapevine as fast as theirs.

'And when you're not here, you're out partying.'

Was it his imagination or was there a hint of jealousy in her voice? 'And you have a problem with that?'

'What you do with your life is your affair. Sorry—*affairs*.' She emphasised the plural. 'And what I do is up to me.'

'Correction,' Seb said crisply. 'You're expecting my baby, so what you do isn't just up to you any more. You're absolutely sure about this?'

'I'm not like you—I don't sleep my way round the hospital!' Alyssa snapped.

He hadn't slept his way round the hospital either. In fact, he hadn't had sex since the night he'd spent with Alyssa. Which was probably why he was in such a vile mood right now. Sheer sexual frustration.

He kept a grip on his temper. Just. 'I wasn't questioning that the baby's mine. I was asking if you'd done a test.'

'Yes.'

'And it was positive.'

'Yes.'

'Which makes you…' He calculated rapidly. 'Six weeks? Seven?'

'Six.'

'Right. Time enough for us to get married before you start to show.'

Her jaw dropped. 'What?'

'You heard. We're getting married.'

Alyssa scoffed. 'This is the twenty-first century. Getting pregnant doesn't mean having to get married any more.'

'It does in my family,' Seb said. 'If I don't do the decent thing, the papers will find out and drag my family name through the mud. I couldn't give a damn about Mara and Barry—but I mind about Charlie and Vicky. I mind a lot.'

'I'll deny it's yours.'

'A paternity test will say otherwise,' Seb countered. 'And then there's the hospital grapevine. Everyone knows you went to Charlie's wedding with me—and there's a photograph in one of the gossip rags of you dancing with me.' Slow dancing. He wished he hadn't brought that up. It made him remember how she'd felt in his arms. Sweet and soft and warm. The way she'd reached up to kiss him, her mouth shy at first and then matching the heat she'd sparked in him.

'Just because I went to the wedding with you, it doesn't mean people will think that I slept with you.'

'But you did,' Seb pointed out. Ah, hell. Their conversation wasn't supposed to be heading this way. He was meant to be getting rid of her obstacles, not fighting her. Not saying things that reminded him of how soft her skin was, the little noises she made when she climaxed, how perfect the weight of her body had felt on top of his. 'We made love, Alyssa.' It *had* been making love, not just having hot, pleasurable sex—though it had been that, too. 'And now you're expecting my baby.'

'I told you. I'm expecting absolutely nothing from you.'

She really thought he wouldn't want to help? That he'd desert her. 'I'm not your father, Alyssa.'

She gave a shocked intake of breath. 'That's a low blow.'

He felt slightly guilty about saying it, but it was still true. And she needed to face it. 'Look, I don't know the full story about your dad. Just that he wasn't around when you grew up—and I'm telling you now, I don't intend to be like that with *my* child.' Being a weekend father wasn't an option either. If he was going to be a dad, he'd do it properly. Full time.

'I'm not getting married to you.'

He remembered what she'd told him about her ex. 'I'm not Scott either,' he said. 'I can assure you now, I don't have any commitments elsewhere. And if I make a promise, I keep it. Forsaking all others and cleaving only unto you.'

She shook her head. 'You hate the idea of settling down with one person. Look at you this past month. You've dated someone different every single day. Sometimes it's been one person for lunch and someone else for dinner!'

She'd noticed?

Not that it was important now. No matter how many women he'd dated, nothing had worked. He'd still found himself thinking about Alyssa instead of his date. Wanting her. And Lord, Lord, Lord, how he'd tried to stop wanting her. He didn't want to settle down, risk his heart with someone.

Though now she was expecting his baby. And that made all the difference in the world.

'I don't need you, Seb. Neither does the baby. We'll be fine on our own. And I don't expect you to contribute anything—financial or otherwise.'

That rankled. 'You seriously think I'd abandon you?'

'I told you because you have a right to know the situation. But that's as far as it goes. I don't want your money. Got that? I'm *not* a gold-digger.'

'I never said you were.'

'But I know you, Seb. I know the way your mind works. I don't want anything from you. I'm handling this myself.'

'Wrong,' he cut in. 'It takes two to make a baby. And two to deal with the consequences.'

Hurt flickered across her face. 'You're expecting me to have a termination?'

Hell, that had come out wrong. He hadn't meant that at all.

He'd meant that they had to pull together, work as a team, and give their baby a good life. 'No. I want you to do the decent thing and give this baby my name.'

'Seb, we're not compatible.'

'Aren't we? Funny, that's not how I remember it.' He couldn't help licking his lower lip. Just as well his desk was between them or he'd be tempted to grab her and kiss her until she stopped arguing with him. Prove to her that there was definite chemistry between them. Remind her of just how good it had been when their bodies had joined.

She lifted her chin, as if she were reading his mind. '*That* was just sex.'

No, it had been more than that. A lot more than that. And he'd been running scared from it ever since. He had the distinct impression that she felt the same. 'Care to verify that statement?' he taunted.

'No.'

He gave her a half-smile. 'Coward.'

Her eyes glittered. 'I'm no coward.'

'Which is why you're going to do the right thing and marry me.'

She shook her head. 'I'm not getting married. Not to you, not to anyone.'

He sighed. 'Alyssa, not all men are scum. I know you've had a rough time—the two men you'd expected to support you, your husband and your father, both let you down.'

'And you seriously think you're any different? Seb, your idea of a relationship is a date, sex and a kiss goodbye.'

'We haven't been on a date,' Seb pointed out. 'The raffle prize didn't count as a date, and neither did Charlie's wedding.' Or lunch the day after the wedding. That had been just a comfort stop on the way home. 'And I haven't kissed you goodbye.' Though he was going to have to try very hard not to think about what had happened in between.

Sex.

Good sex.

Something he most definitely wanted to repeat. And soon.

'We're not having a relationship,' Alyssa insisted.

'We are now.'

She raked a hand through her hair. 'Will you stop being difficult about this?'

'I'm not being difficult. You're having my baby. And that changes everything.'

'It doesn't change a *thing*,' she protested. 'If anyone asks, I'll tell them you wanted to do the right thing and it's my choice not to. I don't want to get married, Seb. Not to you or to anyone else. What do I have to say to make you realise that?'

He'd gone too far. There was a note of desperation in her voice. And stress wouldn't be good for her or the baby. He sighed. 'Alyssa, I'm sorry. Sit down, please. I'll be civilised. But we do need to talk about this.'

'There's nothing more to say.' But, to his relief, she sat down.

'Do you want some water?'

'No, thanks.'

She wasn't going to accept *anything* from him right now. OK. He'd try the softly-softly approach. 'Does your mum still live in Newcastle?'

'Yes.'

'And you live and work in London. Miles away. It's going to be tough, bringing up a baby on your own.'

'She managed.'

'But we're not our parents, Alyssa. We're different people, with our own strengths and wants and needs. Your mum lives a long way away. What happens when your hormones go haywire and you need a cuddle *right now*?'

Alyssa wished he hadn't said that. Because that was what she most wanted right now. Someone to put their arms round her and comfort her and tell her everything was going to be OK. She lifted her chin, trying to brazen it out. 'I'll phone my mum.'

'It's not the same as having someone with you. Someone to hold you. Someone to lean on.'

She knew that. But she'd manage.

'What about antenatal appointments?'

'Most women go to them on their own.' Not the scans maybe…but she didn't want Seb involved. Sure, he'd be fine at first. He'd be an angel throughout her pregnancy. He'd give her foot-rubs and massage her back and get her water and cream crackers when she was feeling queasy. But he'd soon start to feel trapped. Broken nights with a baby, colic, endless feeds and nappy changes—he'd just hate it. He didn't even like dealing with paediatric cases in the department. He'd never cope with having a baby of his own, living with it and being a parent. He'd try—of course he'd try—but just when she'd started to hope they could make a go of it he'd feel trapped and he'd leave.

And she'd be left to pick up the pieces.

No, it was easier not to start what couldn't be finished.

'Who's going to be there to wipe your face when you're sick? To get you dry crackers and tea when you can't face getting out of bed in the morning? To rub your back when the baby's been pressing against your sciatic nerve and your back's aching like hell? To put their hand on your tummy when the baby's kicking and share the moments with you?' he asked.

She didn't meet his gaze. 'I'll manage fine on my own.'

'I know you're perfectly capable of doing that, but you don't have to. I'll be there for you, Alyssa.'

She only wished she could believe him. 'No.'

'You do need something from me, though. Information.'

She frowned. 'Information?'

'Family medical history. Blood groups. That sort of thing.'

He had a point. 'I'll let you know if the midwife has any questions,' she said coolly.

'You're not going to give a millimetre on this, are you?'

'No.' She couldn't afford to. If she leaned on him now, it would only be harder to learn to rely on herself again when he left. She'd been there and done that with Scott. Never again.

'I guess there's nothing more to say, then.'

'No.' And she wasn't going to look into his face. She really didn't want to see the relief at how easily she'd let him off the hook. 'I'd better get back to my patients.'

'Yes. And I have a meeting.'

He didn't even bother to say 'see you around'. Which only went to show how insincere he'd been about being there for her. He just wasn't capable of it. And Alyssa knew that she was doing the right thing. For all of them.

At the end of her shift, Alyssa was surprised to see Seb in the staffroom.

'Are you busy this evening?' he asked.

She frowned. 'Why?'

He sighed. 'We used to be friends. Now I can't even ask you a question without you leaping down my throat.'

Correction. He'd hardly noticed her in his first six months at the Docklands Memorial Hospital. He'd been annoyed that she'd resisted his charm when she'd 'won' the raffle prize of a night out with him; then they'd been working towards friendship of a sort when she'd accompanied him to his brother's wedding.

Then they'd slept together.

And for the last month he'd practically ignored her again. How could he call that being friends?

'All I was going to say,' he said softly, 'is that you look a bit tired. So I wondered if you'd let me cook you dinner tonight.'

'You want to cook me dinner?' The Hon. Sebastian Radley, domesticated? She couldn't imagine it. He *had* prepared that breakfast tray for her—but, then again, he'd mentioned the cook. So he'd probably just handed out orders, like he would in a restaurant, and he hadn't actually prepared it himself.

'Peace offering.' He held both hands up as if in surrender. 'I'm not going to nag you. Or even bring up That Which Must Not Be Talked About.'

Obviously his date for the evening had let him down and he was at a loose end. Well, she didn't want to be second best. 'I'm not very hungry.'

'You need to eat, Alyssa.'

True, but she really didn't feel like cooking. She couldn't handle the smells. A Marmite sandwich and an apple would do just fine.

'All you have to do is sit there with your feet up and sip a glass of iced water with a slice of lemon,' Seb coaxed. 'And I have a dishwasher, so I won't make you wash up afterwards.'

'You're going to cook for me at your place?'

'And I'll give you a lift home after dinner. Or I'll call you a taxi if you've had enough of my company.'

It was tempting. Too tempting. And she was so tired. How could she resist? 'OK. Thank you,' she said quietly.

He drove them back to his flat to the strains of Mozart—

she was glad that he didn't insist on making conversation. When he unlocked his front door, as she'd expected, it was a world away from where she lived. A Docklands waterfront flat. A penthouse flat, to be precise, with a balcony overlooking the Thames. She wouldn't even be able to afford a broom cupboard in his apartment block—a flat this size was beyond the reach of anyone who wasn't earning serious megabucks. Stockbrokers or bankers. Not your average hospital doctor.

'It was bought years ago with trust money, before you say anything,' Seb said. 'I wheedled the trustees into making an investment for me when this block was being built. It paid off.'

'It's very nice,' she said.

Nice? No, it was a dream flat. Airy and light and spacious.

Though there wasn't anything of Seb in it. It felt more like a show flat than a home. Light walls, polished wood floors—and it was real wood, not laminate—classy silk rugs and plush leather sofas. All perfectly complementing each other, and all looking as if a designer had chosen them. Which, knowing Seb, was probably the case: he couldn't be bothered with decorating.

All the electrical equipment was state of the art—a huge plasma TV, a tiny sound system which she recognised as being a top-of-the-market brand, an equally expensive computer system. Real boys' toys. She'd just bet there was a top-of-the-range games console tucked away neatly in the cupboard underneath the TV.

The art on the walls was calculated to be easy on the eye. Watercolours, presumably originals, of river scenes. They were relaxing, yes—but where was the passion? Where was the bright zing of colour that she'd half expected Seb to like? But no. Even in his own home, Seb kept everything at a safe

distance. There was only one photograph on the mantelpiece:
Seb with Charlie and Vicky. Nothing else personal at all.

A baby wouldn't fit in here. This was a suave, sophisticated
adult's place. Definitely not child friendly. Sticky fingers,
spilled juice and a trail of toys wouldn't be welcome here.
Alyssa wasn't too sure that she belonged here either.

'Water.' Seb took two glasses from a cabinet and walked
over to the brushed-steel American-style fridge. He pressed
a button and ice chinked into the glasses. Another press of a
button and chilled water gushed out. He reached into the
fridge and added a slice of lemon to each drink, then handed
one glass to her. 'Take a seat.'

Seb's kitchen was almost half the size of Alyssa's entire
flat. The worktops were granite, the floor was slate, the table,
chairs and cabinets were solid beech, and all the equipment
she could see was brand-new and in the latest fashionable de-
signs and colours. He probably changed his kitchen and ac-
cessories every season. It was a kitchen to die for, but not the
kind of place she'd imagine him to spend time in. Seb liked
restaurants, not home comforts and domesticity—didn't he?

Though when he took a knife from the wooden block,
tested the blade and then proceeded to sharpen it expertly with
a butcher's steel, she realised that this place *wasn't* for show.
Seb did actually know his way around a kitchen. And he
cooked without a recipe book, so he clearly either knew this
recipe well or was confident enough with his culinary skills
to know what went together and in what kind of proportions.

'Want me to leave the garlic out?' he asked.

She nodded. 'Strong smells make me feel a bit…' Hastily,
she took another sip of water. Now was *not* the time to be sick.

'Sure. Chicken OK?'

'Lovely.'

'Dijon or stroganoff?'

'I don't mind.'

'Dijon, then.' He smiled at her and began cooking.

There were herbs growing in terracotta pots on the window-sill, she noticed. Mint, coriander, basil and parsley. Seb broke off a sprig of mint and added it to a pan of baby new potatoes, then chopped an onion at frightening speed.

'Sure you didn't think of being a surgeon?' she asked.

He grinned. 'If you think I'm fast with a knife, you should see Vicky. She's scary. And probably more precise than I am.'

She watched, fascinated, as he prepared the chicken Dijon, put French beans in a steamer and kept an eye on the potatoes.

'It's cream again, isn't it?' she asked as he took a pot from the fridge.

'*Crème fraîche*. And I'll have you know, it's half-fat.' The dimple reappeared briefly.

Oh, Lord. He was so appealing when he did that. It made her want to touch him again.

He'd got rid of his tie at some point and undone the top two buttons of his shirt. She could just see the sprinkling of hair on his chest. A chest that she remembered being perfectly sculpted.

What would he do if she walked over to him and undid the rest of the buttons? Would he pick her up and carry her to his bed? Would he make love to her, the way he'd made love to her at Weston? Sweet and slow, or hot and fast?

Both?

Oh, she really had to get sex off the brain.

But how could she when Seb had such a perfect bottom? His dark suit trousers emphasised his perfect shape. A shape that any woman with red blood would want to touch.

No wonder women fell for Seb in droves. He was delectable.

Yes, they could have sex. Right here, right now. But it wouldn't change things between them. And the more used she got to being with him, the tinier the pieces of her heart would be when it all ended.

Because she knew it definitely would end. Seb didn't believe in for ever.

She blinked back the tears, hardly noticing that he was setting the table, and then suddenly there was a perfectly cooked meal in front of her. Beautifully presented on white china, with a garnish of finely chopped fresh parsley.

'Leave anything you don't want. I won't be offended.'

'Thanks.' She took a mouthful. It was excellent—though why had she expected anything else? Seb did everything well.

Except children.

'It's lovely,' she said.

'Pleasure.'

True to his word, he didn't push her. He didn't say a word about babies or scans or fathers' rights or getting married. He just fed her. Fresh strawberries, to follow the chicken—no cream, just a squeeze of orange juice to bring out the flavour of the fruit—and no coffee. When she explained that she couldn't bear the smell, he elected not to have coffee either. Instead, he made her a cup of tea. Just like he'd made for her the morning when she'd woken in his arms with a hangover.

A morning she'd tried so hard to forget.

He drove her home on exactly the same terms. Waited until she was safely indoors before he drove away. And that was when it hit her. The way he'd cosseted her tonight: it was the way she wanted to be treated. Cherished. But with Seb it wouldn't last. Once the thrill of the chase had worn off, he'd move on.

So this had better be the one and only time she let him do it. Because if she got used to this, it would break her heart when he left.

CHAPTER TWELVE

So MUCH for the softly-softly approach. Seb swore in frustration as he drove home. This was the fourth evening in a row that Alyssa had turned him down when he'd offered to cook for her. He knew his culinary skills weren't at fault—he found cooking relaxing and he was good at it.

No, she was just avoiding him.

Because she didn't trust him.

What did he have to do to prove that he meant it? That he wanted to look after her *and* their baby?

It was so ironic. He'd spent his life flitting from one woman to another, never letting anyone tie him down. Now he'd found the woman who made him want to be different—and she didn't believe in him.

In the end, he rang his sister and asked if he could call round.

'You must be seriously bored,' Vicky said when she opened the door to him. 'Or did your date let you down at the last minute?'

'No. I just thought I'd come and see you.'

Her eyes narrowed. 'Something's happened.'

'No,' he lied.

She gave him a quick hug and ruffled his hair.

'What was that for?'

'Because you're my big brother. Because I love you, even when you're a louse. And because I think, right now, you need it.' She made him a cup of tea just the way he liked it, and placed a tin of biscuits on the kitchen table between them.

'This looks like comfort food,' Seb said. Just what he wanted. Though Vicky had already helped, with that hug. Ha. You were supposed to look after your baby sister, not lean on her. What kind of man was he?

He didn't want to answer that. Instead, he bit viciously into a chocolate biscuit.

Vicky waited until he'd finished before she asked softly, 'Want to tell me about it?'

'No. But what do women *want*, Vic?'

She blew out a breath. 'The fact you're asking is definitely progress. You've moved up the evolutionary scale.'

He folded his arms. 'When you've finished insulting me, perhaps you'd answer the question? I'm serious, Vic. I need to know.'

She thought for a moment. 'What women want depends on the woman.'

He banged his head on her kitchen table. 'That tells me nothing! I'm going crazy here, Vic. I need to know. What do *you* want? Love? Security? Money?'

Vicky shrugged. 'You're asking the wrong woman. I'm a neurosurgeon.'

'And your career comes first.' Same as his had—until Charlie's wedding. Until the night he'd made love with Alyssa. Until he'd discovered that he was going to be a father. 'Yes, I know that.' He waved her protest aside. 'OK, I'm asking *hypothetically*. If you had a life partner, what would you want from said person?'

She thought about it. 'Respect. An equal partnership. Someone I could trust with my life.'

'Do you think that's what she wants?'

'You'll have to ask her that,' Vicky said. 'It's Alyssa, isn't it?'

There was no point in lying. His sister knew him too well. He nodded. 'She won't even have dinner with me. And—' He stopped. He couldn't betray Alyssa's confidence like that. He changed tack slightly. 'Vic, do you think I'd make a good father?'

Vicky's jaw dropped. 'She's pregnant?'

Oh, no. She wasn't supposed to guess that! He shuffled in his seat. 'I didn't say that.'

'Why else would you ask a question like that?'

He shrugged. 'Idle curiosity?'

Vicky scoffed. 'From another man maybe. From someone who claims he's allergic to kids…it means you've just found out you're going to be a dad, and you're terrified.'

'Not in the way you think,' Seb said. 'She says she's going to bring the baby up on her own. As a single parent. Without me.' He raked a hand through his hair. 'I told her I'd marry her, and she said no.'

'Hang on. You *told* her you'd marry her?' Vicky rolled her eyes. 'Seb, you're supposed to *ask*, not bulldoze!'

'Look, I'm a good catch. I'm a consultant, I earn a decent salary, I have a nice flat, I'm good company.' He spread his hands. 'Why wouldn't she want to marry me?'

'Let me see. Because you're never serious about anything other than your work? Because you never date anyone more than once? Because you won't let anyone close? Seb, any woman who has a grain of common sense knows that it's not worth trying to reform you, because you're not reformable. You'll always be a flirt and a tease, and you'll never settle down. You're for fun, not for ever.'

'Supposing I want to change?' he asked.

Vicky stared at him. 'You're in love with her, aren't you?'

'What's love?' he asked.

'Don't play games, Seb,' she warned. 'Do you love her?'

'Yes. And it's driving me out of my mind,' he admitted. 'I can't stop thinking about her. Or the baby. I've never, ever…' Never fallen in love before. Wasn't it supposed to make you feel fabulous? Only he felt bruised and sore. 'Fallen' was about right. He felt as if someone had dropped him from a huge height into a deep lagoon. Belly flop *extraordinaire*. And now he was scrabbling for the surface, trying not to drown.

'Have you told her that you love her?' Vicky asked softly.

'No.'

She sighed. 'You're really in danger of living up to the stereotype posh bloke being like clotted cream.'

'What?'

'Rich and thick,' Vicky explained with a grin. 'She's not a mind-reader, Seb. And you're even better than Charlie is at hiding how you feel. I'd say this has hit you hard. So you've been partying more than normal, right?'

'Right,' he admitted.

'And she probably thinks you're partying because you don't want her, you want constant change and constant fun. The thrill of the chase.'

'It isn't like that.'

'So tell her how you feel. Be honest with her.'

He was going under again. Drowning. Water roaring in his ears. 'What if she still says no?'

'Then you'll have to deal with it. Seb, you can't spend the rest of your life running in case someone rejects you. Not all women are like Mama Dearest. If Alyssa believes you're sincere, you're in with a chance.'

'I only hope,' Seb said helplessly, 'that you're right.'

Vicky took the cup away from him and poured the contents down the sink.

'Hey! I was drinking that.'

'Your cup's empty,' she said. 'No excuses left. Go and see her.'

'What, now?'

'Now.'

Panic set in. 'What do I do? Do I take her flowers? Chocolates?' Seb shook his head in frustration. 'I don't know how to do this, Vic.'

'You don't need flowers. You don't need chocolates. Just be yourself and tell her what you've told me,' Vicky counselled. 'Now, go.'

Seb had coped with major accidents, working late into the night to save victims of a train crash. He'd brought people back from the edge of death when their hearts had stopped. He'd done a surgical cricothyroidotomy at a roadside using the outside of a disposable ballpoint because the tracheotomy tube in the trauma kit had split and the patient would have died if they'd waited for an ambulance to turn up with a replacement kit.

But none of that had been scary. He'd known exactly what he was doing.

This, Seb thought as he drove over to Alyssa's flat, was the first time in his life that he was going into something, knowing he might fail. Exams, driving test—they'd all been easy because he'd been prepared, and he'd always got top marks. Always coasted to the top of the class.

But he couldn't be prepared for this. He had to rely on making Alyssa see that he was serious. That he meant it.

And there was a very, very good chance that she wouldn't believe him.

'Please. Please just let me do this right,' he prayed in a whisper. 'Let her say yes.'

* * *

The doorbell rang and Alyssa woke with a start.

Ow. Bad move, she thought as she crawled off the sofa. Her back hurt like mad. She'd been reading a journal on the sofa and she'd fallen asleep. She *never* fell asleep when she was studying.

Then again, she'd never been pregnant before. Hormones had a lot to answer for.

She wasn't expecting anyone to call round, and her friends didn't tend to drop in without calling first. It could be a neighbour with a parcel maybe, but she wasn't expecting anything.

And nine o'clock on a Wednesday evening was a strange time to call anyway.

It must be a cold caller, then. She kept the security chain on the door and opened the door just enough to explain that, sorry, she wasn't interested, please, go away.

And blinked in surprise as she saw Seb standing there.

'May I come in?' he asked.

'I…er… What do you want?'

'Just to talk to you.'

Oh, no. The last four times he'd tried to get her to have dinner with him she'd found an excuse. The last thing she wanted was him to go on and on about the baby needing to have his name. Especially now, when she was still half-groggy with sleep and all she wanted to do was crawl into bed.

She slapped down the little voice in the back of her head that added, *with him.*

'Seb, I'm really not feeling up to being harangued.'

'I'm not going to hara— Oh, no.' Realisation flittered across his face. 'You were asleep. I'm sorry. I didn't think.'

I didn't think. Yeah, that could be Seb's mantra.

'I'll go away. Leave you to rest.'

He didn't look as if he was about to start haranguing her. He looked miserable, she thought. Lost.

And he'd come to her.

She closed the door and undid the safety chain. He was already walking away when she opened the door again. 'Seb.'

He turned to face her.

'I'm awake now, so you may as well come in.'

'How are you feeling? Do you want me to get you some water?'

'I'm perfectly capable of getting myself some water,' she said, a little more sharply than she'd intended.

He flinched. 'Sorry.'

'Me, too. I didn't mean to snap.' He was only trying to be helpful. This must have been as much as shock to him as it had been to her.

He gave her a half-smile and a hint of dimple. 'Hormones.'

'Yeah.' She ushered him into her living room. When he sat on the sofa, she picked the chair. Sitting next to Seb would be a bad move. She'd be too tempted to ask him to hold her. Just hold her and tell her everything was going to be fine.

When she knew damn well that it wouldn't be.

'So what did you want?' she asked.

He was silent for a long, long time. Then he said, 'I'm not very good at this. So forgive me if I get it wrong. I can't stop thinking about you, Alyssa. You and our baby. I…' He slid off the sofa and dropped to one knee. 'Will you marry me?'

Last time, he'd told her he was marrying her.

This time, he'd actually asked her.

But it still didn't feel right. He hadn't said a word about his feelings.

When Scott had asked her to marry him, it had been all hearts and flowers. Champagne and diamonds. He'd sworn undying love and hadn't meant a word of it. This was the complete opposite. No flowery words, no extravagant promises, no glittering gifts. Just four simple little words. *Will you marry me?*

She was tempted. So tempted.

But Seb hadn't said a word about love.

Which meant he was asking her to marry him because he felt guilty. Because he felt responsible. Because he didn't want the papers to run a story that might embarrass his brother and sister. *Not* because he loved her.

And no way was Alyssa going to tie herself into another marriage where her husband didn't really love her. Where she was just a passing fancy. Where the whole thing could just collapse on her again.

So there was only one answer she could give. 'No. I'm sorry, Seb. It's not going to work.' She folded her arms. 'You said you weren't going to harangue me. I'd like you to go, please.' Go, before she embarrassed them both by bursting into tears. And then he'd feel that he had to comfort her, and— Oh, no. She didn't want to be an obligation. She wanted to be *loved*.

She just didn't think Seb was capable of love.

'And there's nothing I could say that would change your mind?'

Oh, there was plenty. And she knew he'd mean it now. But Seb wasn't cut out for life as a husband and father. He was the eternal playboy. He'd be dating women half his age when he was in his fifties, charming and debonair. 'Nothing,' she said quietly.

A muscle flickered in his jaw. 'Then I'll leave you in peace.'

She followed him into the hall so she could slot the security chain back into place. When she'd done that, she slid down the wall until she was sitting with her chin on her knees and her arms wrapped round her legs.

Forgive me if I get it wrong.

Why did he have to make it so hard for her? Why couldn't he just accept that she was trying to give him the freedom he needed, the freedom to live his life the way he wanted? It was better this way. No disappointments.

All the same, a tear slid down her cheek. And she wished—how she wished—that things could have been different. That she and Seb could do this like a normal couple. Together. Reading all the pregnancy magazines, going to antenatal classes, building a solid foundation of love and trust between them—a foundation that would make their baby's world safe and happy.

But it wasn't going to happen.

There was an uneasy truce between Seb and Alyssa for the next week—luckily, not that many of their shifts coincided.

And then the paramedics radioed in with a crisis case. 'Seven-year-old girl, burns and smoke inhalation. Twenty-five-year-old woman with inhalation.'

As the two most senior doctors there, Seb and Alyssa were both needed in Resus. Which meant working together.

Well, she could do this. She was a professional.

'Which do you want?' Seb asked.

For a moment she was tempted to say 'the twenty-five-year-old'. Just to see if he'd meant it when he offered her a choice. But she knew how much he hated paediatrics cases. What was the point of being petty?

'I'll take the child,' she said.

She could have sworn she saw longing in his eyes. But then she glanced at him again and saw the usual urbane, efficient

Sebastian Radley. She must have imagined it. 'I'll call the burns specialist down,' she added.

The paramedics gave them a full rundown of the history when they brought the patients in. 'She'd lit a candle in the bathroom—she'd wanted to run a bath as a treat for her mum. Except the candle caught the curtains and they went up. She tried to put them out but set herself on fire, too. Mum heard the screams, wrapped her in a towel and put the flames out. Someone else had already called the fire brigade—just as well, as they were both overcome by fumes and the firemen had to carry them out.'

'Loss of consciousness?'

'Not sure how long, or how long they were both exposed. Both conscious when we arrived. We've had them both on oxygen in the ambulance. Mum's got second-degree burns to her hands, daughter's got partial thickness burns to her chest and possibly full-thickness burns to her hands and arms.' The paramedic ran through the analgesia, anti-emetics and oxygen they'd given both patients, plus the crystalloid and colloid they'd given to the girl in the ambulance.

The girl was burned badly enough for Alyssa to see that there were going to be problems. They'd probably need to do an escharotomy—cutting the burned areas down to viable tissue—so that the burned skin wouldn't constrict the girl's breathing as it tightened and healed. Exposure to a fire in an enclosed space, such as a bathroom, usually meant smoke inhalation. There was a possibility of carbon monoxide poisoning, as well as poisoning from any gases released from burning materials during the fire. Soot particles from the fire could also cling to the tiny hairs that lined the airways and usually ferried foreign bodies and irritants out of the respiratory tract, so they couldn't do their job properly any more. The soot could block the small airways.

She was going to have to keep a very close eye indeed on this one.

The burns specialist still wasn't down in Resus. 'Can you page him again, Fliss?' she called.

'Sure,' the nurse said.

'And then see if the mum wants us to call anyone.' Maybe her partner had been out for the evening, or maybe he was working nights. But the woman certainly wasn't well enough to help support the little girl—she needed treatment herself.

Alyssa concentrated on the little girl. Tracheal intubation was the first thing, before her throat started to swell too much. Humidified oxygen next. She checked carefully for any signs of bronchospasm. She kept the fluids in the drip going, too— if the little girl wasn't kept properly hydrated, there was a greater chance of developing pulmonary oedema and then pneumonia.

'Any news yet on the dad?' she asked when Fliss returned.

'I spoke to the mum. She's a single parent. It's just the two of them.'

'OK.' Alyssa blinked back the sudden sting of tears. Now wasn't the time to think about how tough it was to be a single parent. How hard it was to deal with things on your own, without a partner's support.

And then the little girl arrested.

An arrest in a child was bad enough, but when there were the extra complications of burns and inhalation injuries…

'We're not going to lose you, sweetheart,' Alyssa murmured fiercely. 'We're just *not*.' The little girl had just wanted to treat her mum to a special bath with a candle. If they lost her, how would the mum ever be able to forgive herself for not paying attention in the few seconds it had taken for the candle to light and the curtains to catch fire? It was heartbreaking because you couldn't watch a child for every single second of the day. Nobody was a perfect parent. You just did the best you could.

And this was a scenario that could happen all too easily in Alyssa's future. If she didn't save this little girl now, she'd never forgive herself.

She worked on pure instinct, the years of training kicking in and taking over. She knew the drill. Shock, CPR, adrenalin, shock, CPR…

'We're in sinus rhythm,' Fliss called.

Thank God. They'd got the little girl back.

Finally the burns specialist turned up. Alyssa gave him a quick history, and worked with him on the wounds until the little girl was stable enough to be moved to the burns unit. The little girl's mum was well enough to go to the unit and sit by her bed, on strict instructions from Seb to alert the nursing staff if she felt in the slightest bit unwell. He had a quick word with the team himself, to make sure they'd keep an eye on the mum when they did the little girl's observations, to watch for any late-occurring signs of complications from smoke inhalation.

'And you,' he said to Alyssa, 'should have been off duty an hour and a half ago.'

'I couldn't leave my patient until she was stable,' Alyssa said. Surely he wasn't going to yell at her for putting the baby at risk? She hadn't done anything unduly physical and, besides, she wasn't intending to announce her pregnancy to the department until she was at least twelve weeks.

He nodded. 'Come into my office a minute, would you, please?'

She frowned, but followed him. Seb closed the door behind them and indicated to the seat.

'Something I want you to think about,' he said quietly. 'That could have been you.'

Alyssa's mouth tightened. 'Meaning?'

'Not necessarily a fire risk. I mean any major health worry with your child—whether it's bronchiolitis, an allergic reaction, an accident. As a single parent, you'd have to deal with it on your own. And you might be ill yourself and just not be able to deal with it the way you'd want to.' He sighed. 'Why put yourself through it, Alyssa? Why, when I'd be there to support you?'

Because she didn't believe he'd be there.

It must have shown on her face, because he raked a hand through his hair. 'I've learned that not all women are the same. You've shown me that. When are you going to realise that not all men are the same?'

CHAPTER THIRTEEN

ALYSSA didn't say anything, and Seb almost howled with frustration. He clenched his fists and flexed them in an attempt to dispel his tension. 'Alyssa, I know how things must have looked this past month. But I haven't slept with anyone since you. I haven't wanted to.' Now, there was an admission. And he'd told her before how much he liked sex. Surely she'd understand what he was telling her?

Still, she said nothing.

OK, if he had to spell it out to her. 'It's driving me crazy, working with you. I want to touch you, Alyssa. I want to hold you.' His whole body was tingling with need. 'One night isn't enough. It isn't anywhere near enough. We can make this work.'

Still she said nothing.

Softly-softly wasn't working. He'd tried to make allowances for hormones, but it just wasn't working. And he was feeling pretty hormonal himself. So he'd try the other approach.

Caveman.

He took Alyssa's hands, pulled her to her feet and jammed his mouth over hers. The first touch made him shiver. Oh, Lord, he'd wanted this. Wanted it since the morning he'd woken up with her sprawled all over him. Wanted to feel her mouth soften and open under his. Wanted to feel her kiss him back. Wanted her hands sliding round his neck—just like they were now.

She clearly wasn't going to believe whatever he said. So maybe his body could tell her for him. She'd be able to feel how fast, how hard his heart was beating. That would tell her how much he wanted her, needed her—loved her. With every touch of his lips, he was saying, *Be with me.*

And the way his hand snaked between their bodies to cup her abdomen—shielding the place where their baby was growing. Surely she'd know from that he was saying how much he wanted to be part of this whole thing? That he wanted to watch his baby growing inside her, see her body ripening and blossoming, feel their baby kicking in her womb?

His hand slid under her shirt until he touched bare skin.

It was good, but it still wasn't enough. With his other hand he began unbuttoning her shirt. Oh, those curves. The memories were driving him insane. He needed to touch, see if she still felt as soft and warm as he remembered. His hands slid up her sides, moulding her curves, and moved to cup her breasts.

Perfect. She was absolutely perfect.

He loved her perfume. The way she smelt, the way she tasted, the way she felt.

He just loved *her.*

Couldn't she see that? Couldn't she feel that?

Didn't she feel the same? The same desperate rush of heat whenever they were in the same room? The same urgent need to be as close as humanly possible? He needed her body wrapped round his—right here, right now.

He teased her nipple with his thumb and forefinger through the lace of her bra. He loved the way she responded to him, the way her nipple peaked against his fingers. And he wanted to taste her. He tore his mouth away from hers, brushed her jawline with kisses, tracked down over her throat. He didn't bother pulling her bra down, just opened his mouth over one nipple and sucked her through the lace.

She gave a ragged gasp, and he felt her hips tilting towards him. Surrender. *Yes.* She wanted this as much as he did.

He released the button of her trousers. Slid the zip downwards. Caressed the soft swell of her stomach.

I love you. Everything's going to be all right. We can make this work.

He willed her to know it—right now, he wasn't capable of coherent speech. But she had to know how he felt. She had to know this wasn't normal for him. He was the Hon. Sebastian Radley, urbane and cultivated and very much in control.

With Alyssa, he was just wild.

But as his hand slipped beneath the waistband of her knickers to cup her sex, she clamped her hand over his wrist.

'No.'

'No?' He could hardly think straight. His senses were full of her. Of her and their baby and their future.

'No.'

The word echoed into his head. Shocked at realising just how far they'd gone—particularly as he hadn't even locked his door—he jerked his hands out of her clothes and took a step backwards.

Her hands were shaking as she restored her clothing to order.

'Alyssa, I'm sorry. I didn't mean to—'

'Just don't,' she cut in. Her face was flushed and her eyes were over-bright. And her body was most definitely aroused—he'd felt the heat from her sex, and her nipples were clearly visible through her shirt. She wanted him as much as he wanted her.

Or was he reading this entirely wrong?

Right now, he wasn't sure. He wasn't sure of anything, any more. Only that he needed Alyssa. Wanted her. Loved her.

'We're attracted to each other, but it's just sex. What's the point?'

What? 'Alyssa—'

'It's not going to work, Seb,' she cut in.

Before he could gather his scrambled thoughts, let alone marshal a coherent argument to explain to her that he'd fallen in love with her and he wanted her in his life permanently, she'd walked out of his office and closed the door behind her.

And he realised he'd just made the situation ten times worse.

She hadn't heard anything his body had been telling her. She thought he'd been after a quick, easy lay. She thought he'd wanted just sex.

No. He'd wanted *her.* Heart and mind and soul and body. All of her.

Oh, hell. What was it going to take to make her realise he was serious about her?

Words weren't enough, he was sure of it. After her ex-husband, she wasn't going to trust declarations of undying love. Flowers, chocolates, a huge fluffy teddy bear—they wouldn't work either. Gifts were out. Speeches were out. No, it was going to take something really practical to convince her.

And he'd better think of something, fast.

For the next two days, Seb was off duty. The two days after that, Alyssa was off.

She didn't admit to herself how much she missed him. Missed his ready smile, his easy charm. Missed the way his body made her blood heat.

How she'd had the strength to walk away from him, that last time in his office, she'd never know. But it had been for the best. Because it would have been just sex. Enjoyable sex yes—she knew very well that he could make her see stars. Bu still just sex. And she wanted more than that.

So when her doorbell rang on the fourth day, her hear leaped with hope. Seb?

No, of course not. She'd turned him down. He wouldn' ask again.

And it wasn't him—it was someone who looked like him Someone she knew and liked.

'Hello, Alyssa.'

Alyssa undid the chain and opened the door. 'Hello, Vicky.'

'I was just passing, so I thought I'd pop in and say thanks for returning my things.'

Alyssa felt the colour burn her face. Underwear she'd had to borrow because she'd been tipsy and spent the night in Seb's bed. The night they'd made this baby. 'Um. Thanks for lending them to me.'

'Pleasure.'

Please, don't let Vicky be here because Seb had told her about the baby.

Almost as if Vicky had seen the suspicious look on her face she said, 'I meant to pop round before, but I've been fairly busy at work. I was speaking at a conference, and then I had the chance to work with a visiting professor.'

'And the time just vanished.' Alyssa understood. Seb had said how dedicated Vicky was to her job. 'Do you want a cup of coffee?' Alyssa asked, hoping that Vicky would say no. No that she didn't want to be hospitable; just that she really couldn't stand the smell of coffee right now.

Forlorn hope. Vicky gave her a wide, wide smile. 'Thanks I'd love one.'

'Come in and sit down.'

OK. She could do this, she told herself as she went into the kitchen. All she had to do was hold her breath while she shook grounds into the cafetière. Or breathe through her mouth, not her nose, so she wouldn't inhale the scent. Think of cool, clear water. Don't think of—

Too late. She bolted to the bathroom and threw up. When she'd finished, she was aware that Vicky was beside her with a towel and a glass of water.

'Thanks,' she whispered.

'Seb hasn't mentioned any stomach bugs decimating the department. So I assume it's something else—and you need me to get rid of the c-o-f-f-e-e,' Vicky said. 'Go and sit down and I'll sort it out.'

Alyssa tried for humour. 'Hey. I'm supposed to be the host.'

'In the circumstances, I think I can let you off.' Vicky winked at her.

A few minutes later, Vicky joined her in the living room with a glass of water. 'So. What does my brother have to say about this?'

'I'm surprised he hasn't already told you.' Was this why Vicky was really here? Was Seb bringing in the big guns to make her agree to give the baby his name?

'He doesn't tell me everything.' Vicky smiled at her. 'How long?'

'Early stages. Eight weeks or so.'

'So I get to be an aunty for my birthday. Excellent.'

Alyssa blinked. Vicky was pleased? 'You want to be an aunt?'

'Oh, definitely. I have a stock of terrible jokes that need to be passed on to the next generation. Most of them learned from Seb, actually.' Vicky gave Alyssa a sidelong look. 'I assume that you'll be making an honest man of my brother?'

Just what she'd thought Vicky might be leading up to. 'No.'

'Why not?'

'He doesn't like children—and I can't see him giving up his little black book. I say "little",' Alyssa added bitterly. 'It's the size of the London telephone directory!'

'Mmm, he does have the reputation of being a playboy,' Vicky agreed. 'Though I've never seen him fall for anyone before.'

'Because that's not how he works.' Seb didn't let anyone close enough.

'That's not what I meant,' Vicky said quietly. 'I meant, before *you*.'

It took Alyssa a while to work it out. 'Seb's fallen for me? But…we haven't even dated!'

Vicky coughed. 'Babies don't just make themselves.'

If only the earth would open up right now and swallow her. She'd just more or less admitted to Seb's sister that she'd had a one-night stand with him. 'Sex doesn't mean anything to Seb.'

'Normally, I'd agree with you. But you're different. You're The One.'

The One. Alyssa had learned the hard way that *that* was a myth. 'I don't think so.'

'Sophie thinks so, too,' Vicky said. 'We reckon you and Seb would be good for each other. But I know Seb's not exactly uncomplicated—so I don't blame you for chickening out and settling for an easy life.' She set her glass down on the coffee-table. 'You look tired, so I'd better let you get some rest. Thanks for the water.'

'Any time. And thanks for lending me your things.'

'No problem.' Vicky paused at the door. 'Alyssa, even if you don't want Seb in your life, I hope I can come and see you when you have the baby. Meet my niece or nephew.' She looked hopeful. 'And maybe the baby might like to know that there's family out there for him or her. Someone else who'll care, too.'

A family. Just like Alyssa hadn't had.

Her mother had had no choice in the matter—Alyssa's father and grandparents hadn't wanted to be there.

For her baby, it was different. The father *and* an aunt wanted to be there.

Was she chickening out, refusing to give Seb a chance? Was she being selfish, not thinking about how Seb felt or how their baby would feel when he or she grew up and realised that Alyssa hadn't given Seb a chance?

'I'll be in touch,' Alyssa promised.

'Do. And if you need anyone to go with you for antenatal appointments or what have you, just give me a call.'

Alyssa nodded, not trusting herself to speak. There was a huge lump in her throat. She barely knew Vicky, and yet the other woman was acting as if Alyssa were already her sister-in-law. Part of the family.

But she'd already passed up the opportunity. Seb wouldn't make the offer a second time. He was too proud.

And, anyway, Vicky was wrong. Seb didn't love her. It had been just sex. And that incident in his office had been just sex, too.

Ah, hell. I've made such a mess of this, Alyssa thought as she closed the door behind her. And there was someone else she needed to talk to. A call she'd been avoiding.

The phone was answered within three rings.

'Were you sitting on the phone, Mum?' she teased.

'Next to it,' Kathy Ward said, laughing. 'Hello, love. I haven't caught you in for a while. I hope you haven't been working *too* hard.'

'It's just been a bit busy,' Alyssa said. 'Mum, are you sitting down?'

'Ye-es.' Concern radiated through Kathy's voice. 'Why?'

'Um, I have some news. Except I'm not sure how to tell you.'

'Honesty's the best way,' Kathy said. 'Are you in trouble? Do you need me to come down?'

'Yes and no.' Alyssa gulped back the tears. 'Mum, I'm pregnant.'

There was a pause. 'How do you feel about it, love?' Kathy asked gently.

'I don't know. Everything's a mess.'

'I'll ring my boss and get some time off. If I drive down first thing in the morning—'

'No, you don't need to do that,' Alyssa protested. 'I'm fine. I just…wanted to talk to you about it.'

'You know I'm always here for you.' Kathy paused. 'What about the baby's father? Or haven't you told him yet?'

'He said we'd have to get married. I said no.'

'Do you love each other?' Kathy asked.

'It's…complicated.'

'He's married?'

'Not *that* sort of complicated,' Alyssa said dryly.

Kathy sucked in a breath. 'Sorry. I didn't mean to bring back bad memories. Do you love him?'

'Yes.'

'But you don't think he loves you.'

She wasn't sure that Seb was capable of loving anyone. At least, not the way she wanted to be loved. 'He doesn't like kids. I don't think he'd be able to cope with a baby.'

There was another pause. 'Do you want to keep the baby?' Kathy asked.

'Yes. I know it's not going to be easy—but I don't want a termination.'

'I'll be there to help you,' Kathy promised. 'I just know I'm going to love this baby as much as I love you. And it's not that far from Newcastle to London—I can babysit and have special days out with my granddaughter or grandson.'

Her mother actually sounded pleased. Not angry. Not as if Alyssa had completely screwed up her life. Pregnant and without a partner. Just as Kathy herself had done.

'If it makes it any easier for you, I never regretted having you,' Kathy said, as if guessing what Alyssa was thinking. 'Not for a moment.'

'Thanks, Mum.'

'But there were times when I wished I'd had someone with me,' Kathy said. 'Someone who'd be there to share the good times—your first smile, your first tooth, your first word, your first step. And someone to hold my hand when you were ill and I was scared.'

Exactly what Seb had offered.

Someone. A family. Like Sophie's huge family, all there and all mucking in together at the wedding. The kind of family Alyssa had never had. The kind of family she couldn't offer her baby on her own.

'Don't judge everyone by your father and Scott,' Kathy said softly. 'And he might surprise you—he might be able to cope better than you think. Some people really don't like other people's kids, but it's different when it's your own.'

'I got it wrong last time, with Scott,' Alyssa said. 'How do I know if it's going to work out this time?'

'There aren't any guarantees in life, love. But there's one acid test. Would you trust him with your most precious possession?'

She'd already trusted him with two secrets. Neither of which he'd told. Vicky had more or less asked if she'd told Seb yet, so he couldn't have told his sister she was pregnant. Vicky hadn't mentioned Scott either.

So could Alyssa trust him with her most precious possession—her heart?

Maybe.

'Only you know the answer to that, Alyssa. But I love you. And if you need me to move down to London, I will. I'll help you as much as I can with the baby.'

'Thanks, Mum. But you don't need to move. I'll cope.'

'I know, but the offer's still there. Just don't close any doors. Don't let pride get in your way.'

Was that what her mother had done?

You couldn't change the past. Only the future. But right now she didn't want to think about the future.

'I'd better go, Mum. But I wanted to tell you about the baby.'

'I'm glad you did. And congratulations, love.'

'Thanks.' Congratulations, Alyssa thought as she put down the phone. Congratulations. So why did she feel like crying?

'Give her space.' That was Charlie's advice. 'Don't push her into a corner. Let her come to you when she's ready.'

But what if she never did?

It had been four days since Seb had seen her. And he was slowly going crazy.

This was bad. It had never, ever happened before.

'That's love for you,' Charlie said with a grin.

'Well, thanks for nothing, brother mine,' Seb said, scowling. He couldn't go on like this. It would drive him insane.

How was he going to convince Alyssa that he was serious about her? What would make him seem the steady, dependable type?

Selling the flat? If she wanted a house with a garden for the baby, fine. He'd get a swing and a slide and a trampoline, too. And they'd have a nursery with a big wooden rocking horse. Strictly speaking, the rocking horse at Weston belonged to Charlie, but Seb was pretty sure that his brother would be a doting uncle and at least lend it to them for a little while. Or maybe they could buy a new one just for their children.

The car would have to go, too. They'd need something solid and sturdy, with a properly anchored baby seat. He'd miss the E-type, yes—but it was a small price to pay. Classic car or the woman he loved? No contest.

Because this was going to be his future. A proper home and a proper car and a wife and children. All the glitter and the parties and the air-kissing—actually, he wouldn't miss them either. Because he'd have something real. Someone who loved him for himself.

He'd prove to Alyssa that he was worthy of her. And he'd propose to her again. And this time, please, God, she wouldn't say no.

CHAPTER FOURTEEN

THE hospital grapevine was really buzzing.

Seb was selling his E-type.

And there were plenty of theories why. He'd lost a fortune at a casino and needed some cash fast. He was trading it in for a seriously fast motorbike. He'd reached the top of the list for having a new hand-built Aston Martin. He'd been sponsored by a car manufacturer to drive something else.

Alyssa didn't bother joining in with the speculation. It wasn't any of her business whether Seb was selling his E-type.

But then she heard he was selling his flat as well—and that hurt. Rumour had it that the real reason why he was selling the E-type and his flat was he'd got a prestigious new job abroad. Yeah, she could see that. He was ambitious and bright enough to get any job he wanted. And he had an extra reason for wanting to go: to get as far away as he could from what other people would consider his responsibilities. The baby—and her.

Which just went to prove that she'd been right not to trust him.

His guardian angel was definitely looking after him today, Seb thought. His first case that morning was a paediatric one—absolutely perfect for helping him get over his problem with dealing with kids.

Though this one was a nightmare. The little boy was almost hysterical because he had a bug in his ear. He could hear it crawling about and he could feel it and he was convinced it was going to eat through his head.

Seb would have to be careful. If he used a rigid instrument to get the bug out of the little boy's ear, one unexpected movement could cause serious injury to the middle ear. And Seb definitely couldn't remove a bug without killing it first—the bug would put up a fight, and the noise would terrify the little boy. Again, there was a risk of damage to the ear canal.

The noise of a fly buzzing in your ear was enough to upset an adult, let alone a kid. And it was made worse because this little one believed that the fly was going to take a bite out of him.

'Absolutely not,' Seb said reassuringly. 'Flies don't eat people.'

'My brother says they do. They eat your brains and you turn into a zombie.'

'I promise, they don't eat people.' Seb would have liked to strangle this little one's brother. 'How old's your brother?'

'Thirteen.'

Just at the age when he wouldn't want to be bothered with a four-year-old. So he'd gone for the 'give the kid nightmares and he'll go away' approach. Great.

Now Seb had to calm the child down before he could sort out the problem. But how? What did small boys like?

When Seb had been four, he'd been fascinated by worms and spiders.

Spiders. That was it. Spiders ate bugs. Maybe this would work… 'Guess what? I've got some magic stuff that will stop the bug doing anything to you.'

'Magic stuff?'

There was only a flicker of interest through the fear, but it was enough. Magic. Seb smiled. 'Mmm-hmm. Special magic potion called…' Oh, God, he had to think of something spidery, and fast. 'Spider potion.' Please, please, let that sound magic enough.

'What does it do?'

'It magics the bug out of your ear. So then you won't hear it or feel it or anything. And the spider potion will magic you all back to normal.'

'And it won't eat my brain?'

'It won't eat your brain,' Seb reassured the little boy. 'I think Mummy might be having a chat with your brother later, to explain that to him, too.' He gave the little boy's mother a speaking look.

'I had no idea,' she mouthed back. 'I thought he was just upset because of the thing in his ear.'

Ha. Ordinarily, Seb would have focused on the mum rather than the child. Especially as he had a weakness for blondes—and this one had long blonde hair and a very kissable pout.

Except what he really wanted was a pair of sea-green eyes, short chestnut hair and a much, much more seductive mouth. A mouth that made his blood sing even when it was flaying him.

So Seb concentrated on his patient.

'What's your name?' Seb asked the little boy.

'Mikey.'

'Mikey, I'm going to take a look in your ear with a special torch so I can see where the bug is and how much magic potion to put in. Is that OK?'

'It's buzzing. I don't like it.'

'All right. I'll be really quick, promise,' Seb said. 'You're being really brave, Mikey.' He took a look in the little boy's ear. As he'd expected, the auriscope showed a small black fly.

'OK, we're going to do the magic now. What I need you to do is lie on your side, with your buzzy ear towards me, while your mummy holds your hand. Can you do that?'

Mikey nodded and his mother helped settle him.

'Superstar. Now you say a magic word.'

'Abracadabra?'

'Brilliant. And close your eyes—the magic works best if you close your eyes.' And Mikey wouldn't see the pipette of olive oil and panic. 'You'll feel the magic potion going in drop by drop,' Seb explained. Simple olive oil, which would suffocate the bug and make it easy to remove. 'But I'm going to need to pull on your ear flap here just a little bit,' he said, putting Mike's ear flap between his finger and thumb. 'It won't hurt you, but I need to do that to make the magic work.' If you didn't put tension on the ear flap, air bubbles could get into the oil.

'Then I have to put my special spider potion wand in—it looks like a syringe to you and me, but there isn't a needle in it. It's the second part of the special spider potion.' Also known as warm water. As long as the bug wasn't tightly wedged, it would be flushed out—a technique Seb wouldn't use with anything like a bean or a seed, because it would cause the vegetable matter to swell and make it harder to remove. If the water didn't work, he could use suction, but he really didn't want to use forceps unless he really had to. Invasive techniques could scare children, and he didn't want to risk any inner-ear damage. Even if forceps worked, they tended to make the ear bleed and both the child and the parent would be frightened.

The important thing was to keep the child calm and cooperative. The magic idea seemed to be working. So he'd take it one step further. How had Alyssa kept the kids entertained at Charlie's wedding? Stories. He wasn't any good at stories. Songs?

Songs.

'What you have to do is sing me a song about bugs to make the magic work even more. Do you know any songs about bugs?'

'No,' Mikey quavered.

Seb could only remember one nursery song: 'Old MacDonald'. 'I know one. I bet you'll know it, too. Want to sing it with me to help the magic work?'

'All right,' Mikey said.

There was a wonderful tenor in one of the cubicles singing 'Old MacDonald Had a Farm'. Except the words were different. 'And on that farm he had a fly, ee-I-ee-I-oh. With a buzz buzz here…'

Alyssa wasn't aware of anyone leaving the department, so it had to be either a parent or a locum. One who was good with kids, by the sound of it. Singing was an excellent distraction technique. Fabulous voice, too.

But during the next verse there was a pause, then a voice said, 'A butterfly? What noise does a butterfly make?'

'I don't know,' a child's voice said.

'I reckon it's a flutter,' the adult said decisively. 'Because butterflies flutter by.' The singing began again. 'A flutter flutter here…'

Seb?

No, she must be hearing things. The voice had *sounded* like Seb's, but she knew he'd never take a paediatric case from choice. And it would never occur to him to sing to a terrified child.

But when the cubicle curtain twitched back and she saw Seb presenting the little boy with a special bravery sticker, she could have cried. This was the kind of man who'd make an excellent father.

Except he'd already given up on her and their baby. He was leaving.

She would have slipped silently into one of the cubicles to let him pass without comment, but he'd already spotted her. Gave her that slow, charming smile that was calculated to melt her heart. 'Morning, Alyssa.'

'Morning.' She forced herself to smile back. 'I hear congratulations are in order.'

'Congratulations?'

'Your new job.'

His eyes widened. 'The grapevine here is terrifyingly efficient.'

So he really *was* leaving. Going abroad. 'America, isn't it?'

'America?' He frowned. 'Er, no. And it's not actually a new job as such. It's job enrichment.' His frown deepened. 'I need to talk to you. In private. My office?'

She was still too surprised by the news that he *wasn't* leaving to say anything, so he took her hand and tugged her over to his office. He closed the door behind them, gestured to her to take a seat and leaned back against the door. 'What makes you think I'm leaving?'

'You're selling the E-type and your flat.'

'Well, obviously.'

It wasn't obvious to her. 'Why?'

'I need a better car. Safety-wise, I mean. Something you can put a baby seat in.'

A baby seat? Was he planning to contest her for custody?

'And the flat doesn't have a garden. I need somewhere to put a swing and a slide.'

Oh, no. This sounded as if he *was* intending to go for custody. 'B-but…you don't want kids,' she said shakily.

'I didn't. I've never been good with them. But it's different now. I'm going to be a father. Even if you refuse to put my name on the birth certificate, you're still having *my* baby.' He lifted his chin. 'And, yes, that's why you've heard that I'm changing my job. I'm trying to set up some job enrichment— so we get experience in other departments, and they get experience here. It's a win-win situation. We get to know the issues in other departments, and they get to know the problems we face. So we work better as a team.'

It was a brilliant idea. And Seb had enough charm and determination to push it through all the right channels.

But… 'Have you told anyone about the baby?' she asked suspiciously.

'N— Sort of. I didn't actually *say* it. But the person I was talking to guessed.'

Alyssa's eyes widened. 'Who?'

'Vicky.' He raked a hand through his hair. 'It's OK. She's completely dependable. She won't breathe a word until… What?' His eyes narrowed. 'Problem?'

'When did you tell her?'

'She *guessed*,' he corrected her.

'When?'

He sighed. 'Just before I made a mess of asking you to marry me.'

'But— She didn't say a word to me. She—'

'She told you she wanted to be an aunty and to see the baby when it's born. I know. She told me.'

What else had Vicky told him?

The question must have shown on her face, because he closed his eyes for a moment. 'Alyssa, I'm not perfect. Neither are you. It isn't an issue.'

She raised an eyebrow. 'It is, if you go running to someone else every time things get sticky between us.'

'So what am I supposed to do? Flounder around and make things worse?' Seb shook his head, clearly frustrated. 'All I asked her was what women wanted.'

'And now you know?'

'No. But I'm willing to find out. If you'll help me.'

She wasn't sure she was ready to answer that. 'So what's this enrichment programme?' she asked.

'We're starting with paediatrics, and I'm going to do the trial,' he said. 'It's about time I learned how to deal properly with kids. But for me it's more than a job. It's going to be life enrichment, too. By the time our baby arrives, I'm going to be a bit better with kids and I'm not going to be a complete failure as a father.' He held her gaze. 'I'm going to be there for our baby. And that's why I want an ultra-safe family car and a house with a garden.'

He really meant it. Their baby meant more to him than his most precious possession: his E-type. And even though he loved overlooking the river—he'd told her how water calmed him—he was prepared to give up all that, too.

So Seb was finally facing his demons. He really meant it about wanting to be a good father to their baby.

But why did it have to be at her expense? 'I can't match you financially. I know that. But I'm not going to let you take the baby away from me.'

He stared at her. 'I'm not trying to take the baby away from you. Why on earth do you think I would?'

'You're making all these life changes.'

'Because it's time I grew up. I'm thirty-two.' He shrugged. 'I can't spend the rest of my life behaving like a medical student—no responsibilities, no strings.'

He still thought she was a gold-digger? 'I've already told you, I'm not expecting anything from you. I'm not trying to trap you into anything.'

'I *know*. I'm doing it because I want to. I want to be a good father.'

'You said you never wanted children.'

'People change.'

She wasn't so sure. Her eyes narrowed. 'You've always avoided working with children.'

'I know. They reminded me too much of…' He grimaced and raked a hand through his hair. 'Ah, hell. This is going to sound bad. But you, of all people, have a right to know. I was always a nuisance when I was a kid. Charlie was the heir, and he had a special bond with Dad. Vicky was a girl, and Mara— well, Mara was stupid enough to think that meant having a daughter who'd love ballet lessons and ponies and finishing school and being a debutante. Vic was a born doctor and she wasn't going to put up with it, but it didn't stop Mara trying.'

'And you were in the middle and you felt left out?'

'That makes me sound like a spoiled brat.' He sighed. 'But, yes, I always felt like the odd one out. I didn't fit in. Which was another reason why I didn't ever want kids—I didn't want them to feel they weren't important, that they never came first.'

Just as she'd suspected.

'Don't get me wrong. I'd lay down my life for Charlie or Vic. Anyone who hurts them has *me* to deal with.'

There was a dangerous glint in his eyes. 'Seb, I think you're scaring me.'

He grimaced. 'Sorry. It's the way I feel. The people I love are important to me, but I'm not good at showing it. Well, not at showing it in the right way.' He sighed. 'I'm going to be an awful father. If we have a girl, I'll interrogate every boyfriend. If we have a boy, I'll be doing background checks on his girlfriends. Control freak doesn't even begin to come into it.'

His self-deprecation disarmed her. Particularly as she knew

it was sincere, not meant to manipulate her. 'Seb. People have to learn for themselves, make their own mistakes. And I think you're going to be better than you give yourself credit for.'

'Am I?'

Yes. He was prepared to give up the trappings of his bachelor life for their child. And, OK, so he didn't want her…but he wanted to be there for their child. And she didn't want their child growing up and resenting her for not letting Seb be part of their lives, the way Seb resented his mother.

Seb was trying to give. It was her turn to give now. 'I have a dating scan at four,' she said quietly. 'Do you want to come and see our baby?'

His eyes widened. 'Did you just say *our* baby?'

'Uh-huh.'

'So this means you'll acknowledge me as the baby's father?'

'You told me once that you're not my father and you're not my ex. You're right. You've got more integrity than you think you have.'

But still not enough for her. What was it Vicky had said women wanted? *Respect. An equal partnership. Someone I could trust with my life.* What had he done? Flitted from one woman to another. Treated them as commodities. Not the stuff of equality or respect or trust. Even though it *had* been mutual: he'd never, ever pushed anyone into making love with him. 'I've dated—slept with—a lot of women.' And, now he saw himself through Alyssa's eyes, he despised himself for it.

'You said there hasn't been anyone since me.'

Seb closed his eyes and leaned his head back against the door. 'I don't want anyone else,' he muttered. 'If I can't have you, then it's either abstinence or my own right hand.'

'Seb!'

He opened his eyes and saw how shocked she looked. 'Sorry. I didn't mean it to sound that crude. I like sex, Alyssa. I like it a lot. But it's meaningless without I—' Oh, no. He couldn't tell her *that*. But the look on her face told him he wasn't going to get away with it. So he may as well admit part of it. Enough to stop her probing any deeper. 'I've never felt like this about anyone before, Alyssa. And it scares the hell out of me.' He took a shuddering breath. 'I'll never try to take our baby from you. I just wish you'd—well, want me in your life as well.'

'You want to be part of my life? Not just the baby's?'

Wasn't it obvious? Did she really not know how he felt about her? Didn't selling his car and selling his flat tell her how serious he was about her? 'I ache with wanting you. And it's not just the sex. I need you near me.' Ah, hell. He'd gone this far. If he was going to scare her away, he may as well do it properly and tell her the whole lot. 'I love you. And I've never, ever said that to a woman before.'

He didn't dare look at her, knowing that this was the moment when she was going to push him away. After all, how could she have room for him in her heart now she had the baby to think about?

But when she said nothing, he risked a quick glance. And he saw that she was crying.

Unable to help himself, he walked over to her chair, dropped to his haunches and put his arms round her. 'Alyssa, don't cry. I'm not going to force you into anything.'

She sniffed. 'I'm not crying. It's my hormones.'

She hadn't pushed him away yet. Did that mean…? He took a chance and kissed her tears away. 'Alyssa. Be with me,' he begged softly.

'Be with you?'

'As…' Oh, why was this so hard?

Because she'd refused him twice. He'd told her they were getting married. She'd said no. Then he'd *asked* her. She'd still said no.

Maybe he'd asked the wrong question. 'As my life partner.'

'Not marriage.'

He wasn't sure if it was a question or a statement. 'You've turned me down twice. So it's pretty obvious you're not going to say yes if I ask you again. And marriage—well, it's just a symbol. A piece of paper. You can tear it up. But you can't tear *this* up.' He took her hand and put it over his heart. 'I'm always going to feel this way about you. You're the one who makes me want to be more than just a—well, a shallow playboy.'

Her other hand covered his. 'You're not a shallow playboy, Seb.'

Not any more. Something round his heart was cracking. Unlocking the deep, scary space that had been there for so long. Waiting for her to fill it.

'So does that mean you've changed your mind and you *will* marry me?'

'I don't want a big society wedding.'

Please let that mean yes. 'You don't have to have a big wedding. You don't have to wear a meringue dress or tie up hundreds of bundles of sugared almonds or anything. It can be just you and me in the middle of some remote Scottish island, if that's what you want.'

'You'd give up the media circus for me?'

'In a nanosecond.' And he meant it. 'It doesn't mean anything without you. Nothing does. Just you—me—and our baby.' His free hand reached out to stroke her stomach—then he remembered where he was and what had happened last time he'd touched her in his office and snatched his hand back. 'Sorry. I'm trying to keep my hands off you. And our baby.'

Alyssa couldn't stand seeing the misery in his eyes. He'd offered her his heart. And, unlike Scott, Seb meant every word of it. He wanted her to share his life. And he was trying not to push her into something he didn't think she wanted.

She took his hand and placed it back on her abdomen. 'You do know it'll be about another three months before we can feel the baby kick?'

Seb said nothing. But she could feel him shaking.

'Seb?'

'I never dreamed...' His voice was hoarse with emotion. 'I never thought I'd feel anything like this. I didn't think it existed. Even—well, even after Charlie and Sophie. But now I know. Oh, God. Now I know. It scares the hell out of me.'

She raised his hand to her mouth and kissed it. 'Me, too. It wasn't supposed to happen like this. I wasn't supposed to fall for a playboy who believed in one date, sex and a kiss goodbye.'

'We still haven't officially dated. I have no intention of kissing you goodbye.' His lips quirked. 'I'm not making any promises about sex, though.'

Her gaze met his, and her temperature rocketed several degrees. 'Seb. Not here. We can't.'

'We could,' he whispered. 'All I have to do is lock the door. And then it's just you and me. The couch.'

'Seb, we're on duty.'

'And I'm going crazy with need here. Do you know how long it is since we've made love?' He shuddered. 'OK. Just promise me you'll spend tonight with me. My bed. Or yours, if you'd rather. I really don't care, just as long as I'm with you.' His eyes scorched her. 'But mine's king-sized.'

She grinned. 'Did you know they call you Six-times-a-night Seb?'

The heat in his eyes turned to amusement. 'That's a bit of an exaggeration. Though I think, with you, that wouldn't be enough. I don't think I'll ever be able to get enough of you.' He tipped his head to one side. 'Did you mean it? You've really fallen for me?'

She nodded. 'And you've fallen for me?'

'I've never, ever felt anything like this before. It's as if someone chucked me over a waterfall. And I warn you now, I need a lot of TLC. A *lot* of kissing better.' He nuzzled her ear. 'Kissing better in a *lot* of places.'

Mmm, and she knew just where they could start. 'Sounds good to me.' Even to her own ears, her voice sounded husky. Drenched in sex.

That was what Seb did to her.

He sucked in a breath. 'So what happens now?'

Apart from ripping each other's clothes off and going wild? 'Hopefully our child will have something that neither of us had. Two parents who love each other and are still together when they're ninety. Two parents who *both* love their child.'

'I'm going to make mistakes,' he warned. 'I'm very far from being perfect.'

She shrugged. 'You're human. Anyway, you learn from your mistakes.' Her mouth twitched. 'You'll only put the nappy on back to front once.'

'I'll change nappies. I'll be there for our child—our children,' he corrected. 'And I'll be there for you.'

'That's all I want,' she said softly.

EPILOGUE

AT FIVE minutes past four, Alyssa was stretched out on the bed, her abdomen exposed and covered in radioconductive gel. Seb was by her side, holding her hand. A bit too tightly, but she wasn't going to complain. Because he was *there*.

And then the screen flickered into life.

'That's our baby,' Seb said softly.

The radiographer ran through the measurements of the head, abdomen and length. She pointed out the tiny black pulsing blob that was their baby's heart. 'All looks absolutely fine. You're about eight and a half weeks.' She smiled. 'Would you like a photograph?'

'Oh, yes, please,' Seb breathed. 'Our baby's first picture.' He looked at Alyssa as she wiped the gel from her stomach. 'We're going to have to buy a baby book this weekend.'

She laughed. 'And, knowing you, you'll scan this in to your computer and use it as a screensaver.'

'As well as keeping a copy in my wallet. Do you mind?'

No. She loved the idea that he wanted a photo of their baby with him. 'So you're going to tell the whole department?'

'No. *We* are—together. When you're ready,' he said quietly.

The radiographer handed him the photograph. Reverently, Seb's fingers brushed the surface. 'Our baby.'

Was it her imagination, or were there tears in his eyes?

He was quiet as they left the ultrasound suite. Too quiet. He didn't say a word until they reached his car. When he'd climbed in beside her, he rested his forehead on the steering-wheel. 'I didn't think love stretched like that. That there would be room for you *and* the baby in my heart.'

She understood immediately what he was trying to say. There hadn't been room for him in his mother's heart—or his father's. And he was scared the same thing would happen to her. She reached out to stroke his hair. 'Seb, love stretches. I'm going to love our baby. And I'm always going to love you.'

'Maybe.'

She frowned. 'Don't you believe me?'

He lifted his head to look at her. 'I want to.'

But he was scared. Just as she was. Maybe it was time to be brave. 'You told me once you don't make promises. Perhaps it's time you did.'

'What sort of promise?'

'Love, honour and cherish. That sort of promise.'

It took a moment for it to sink in. Then he pulled her into his arms and kissed her. 'Yes. And it's going to have to be soon. Before you change your mind.'

She smiled. 'I'm not going to change my mind.'

'Good, because this is going to be for keeps.'

And she knew it would be.

Welcome back to the exotic land of Zuran, a beautiful
romantic place where anything is possible.

**Experience a night of passion
under a desert moon in**

Spent at the sheikh's pleasure…

Drax, Sheikh of Dhurahn, must find a bride for his brother—
and who better than virginal Englishwoman Sadie Murray?
But while she's in his power, he'll test her wife-worthiness
at every opportunity….

TAKEN BY
THE SHEIKH
by Penny Jordan

Available this February.
Don't miss out on your chance to own it today!

They're tall, dark...and ready to marry!

If you love reading about our sensual Italian men, don't
delay—look out for the next story in this great miniseries!

THE ITALIAN'S
FORCED BRIDE
by Kate Walker

Alice knew Domenico would never love
her back—so she left him. Now he is
demanding that she return to his bed.
And when he finds out she's pregnant,
he might never let her go....

Available this February.

Also from this miniseries, coming up in April:
SICILIAN HUSBAND, BLACKMAILED BRIDE
by Kate Walker